BLACK TIGER

THE STORY OF A FAITHFUL HORSE

by
THOMAS C. HINKLE

THE CHILDREN'S PRESS
LONDON AND GLASGOW

This Impression 1970

CONTENTS

CHAPTER ONE

THE CAPTURE

IT WAS late in the afternoon of a summer day on John Sheridan's ranch in the days of the old West. Two of Sheridan's men, Jim Summers and Buck Davis, were riding together along the foot of a high, steep hill. Their horses, a bay and a black, kept their heads up and their eyes forward, as if they had a notion something interesting might be seen at any moment. Just a little ahead there was a cut in the hill. Buck and Jim knew that on the other side of the hill, near the cut, there was a ledge of overhanging rock which would serve to conceal them while they used the spot just below it as a lookout.

They rode into the cut, dismounted, and started to lead their horses up to the rocky ledge curving sharply around the hill. Walking slowly and sweeping their eyes over the valley, they saw, at first, no sign of the famous old outlaw mare and her colt that they were looking for. As they led their horses carefully around the hill and under the overhanging ledge of rock, the men suddenly stopped and looked. A short distance away, they saw the mare and her colt grazing near the deep draw.

Jim Summers, the youngest cowboy on the ranch, had named the colt Black Tiger because of his colour and because of the speed and spirit which had kept him a free creature all the days of his young life, in spite of the efforts that had been made to catch him.

It was John Sheridan who had given the cunning old mare the name of Old Snorter, by which she was known to the whole countryside. As he put it, " She gives the daggondest, loudest snort of any horse on the range when she catches sight of a man."

Like her colt, Old Snorter was a solid coal-black. No one knew just when the colt had been born, but it must have been in the fall, because this spring he had shed his coat and revealed his black colour.

Some years before, Old Snorter had escaped from the ranch and had run wild and free ever since. She had sometimes been noticed in the company of wild horses, but generally when she had a colt she was seen alone with her offspring, as she was now. As Old Snorter grazed, she raised her head now and then and looked sharply all around her, sometimes glancing up towards the top of the hill.

Tiger was truly a wild colt, for he had been born in the wild and no man's hand had ever touched him. He was probably about eight or nine months old, having shed his first coat in the spring, as fall colts do. Like a growing boy, Tiger was always hungry, for his rapidly developing young body needed food almost constantly.

Peeping round the rocky wall, Jim and Buck watched both mare and colt grazing on a patch of green grass near the deep draw, which at this season had only a little water flowing along its bed.

Jim and Buck had worked all morning trying to get close enough to the mare and her colt so that they could rush upon them suddenly from cover and succeed in throwing a rope over the colt's head, even if they could not rope Old Snorter. But, although they had been trying for hours and had a slight wind in their favour, this was the first time they had managed to get as near as this to the watchful old mare and her son.

Both Jim and Buck were tall, lean, and sun-tanned. Jim was the youngest of the men on the Sheridan ranch by several years. He was especially eager to get the colt, because one evening a month ago, at the ranch-house, John Sheridan had said in the presence of all the men, " Fellers, if we ever get that colt he's Jim's. I knew Jim's daddy and I've known Jim since his daddy first set him on a horse to ride when Jim was five years old."

Although Jim was only nineteen years old, he could ride even the worst horses as well as the older and more experienced men could. Like them, he was cool, watchful, and brave in any kind of dangerous situation. Not only John Sheridan, but every cowboy on the ranch, had a deep affection for young Jim.

As Buck and Jim peered from their hiding-place, Buck whispered, " Daggone it, Jim, there's your colt if we can only get him. I reckon we're closer to him and his old mammy than any of the other fellers have ever been. But there's only the two of us. We've got to get closer still or we won't get him."

Some time before, Jim and Buck had noticed a storm cloud in the northwest, which had now grown big and dark and was coming up fast. They knew it was full of thunder, lightning, and drenching rain, but to these hard-riding men a storm, no matter how severe, was just a part of the day's work. Buck and Jim were sure they would be caught in it. By a lucky accident they were here under the jutting ledge of rock, which would give them some kind of shelter. But they did not care whether or not they had any protection at all from the storm if only they could catch the jet-black colt, now that at last they had succeeded in getting so near to him. Both men wanted very much to capture him, but Jim, of course, was particularly eager. He had already shortened the little fellow's name to Tiger, in happy anticipation of the time when he would own him and find it handier to call him by the shorter name. With such a thought in mind, the prospect of driving rain, thunder, and lightning seemed like nothing. On rare occasions, to be sure, a rider caught out in a storm was struck by lightning. But that danger, too, was accepted calmly by the men, in their line of duty as riders of the wild range country.

When the sky began to grow dark and a peal of thunder rumbled across the sky, Buck said quietly, " That storm's about here, Jim. Maybe Old Snorter and her colt will run past us here. Let's get on our horses and have our ropes ready."

Buck mounted, and Jim did also. Each took his coil of rope from the saddle, in order to be prepared if the mare and her colt should gallop past them in search of shelter.

But something unexpected happened. Old Snorter threw up her head, snorted loudly, and then, instead of running, leaped up the steep little bank above the draw, with Tiger close on her heels. A narrow opening, or cleft, in the bank provided a fair shelter for the two horses, and there they stood. It would have served to protect them against any ordinary rain.

As the storm rushed down from the northwest, the great black cloud, shot through with streaks of forked lightning, quickly overspread the sky, and the day grew ominously darker. Jim and Buck could hear the distant roar of the coming rain grow louder and louder. Amid ear-splitting crashes of thunder and blinding flashes of lightning, they dismounted and stood under the ledge of rock, holding their horses by the bridle reins. Neither tried to speak to the other, for the roar of the storm was deafening.

In the cleft of the steep bank, Tiger stood as close to his mother as he could get. The rain beat upon them in such a flood that from time to time the two horses snorted, to blow away the water that dashed against their nostrils.

The draw below had little water in it as yet. On the side nearer the hill the bank rose steeply. On the other side the ground sloped up, but rather sharply, to the level high land. The bed of the draw was deep, so that when a heavy rain fell along its upper reaches, the water came down in a swift rushing flood. Earlier in the afternoon a great deluge had fallen in the upper course of the draw before the storm reached the place where the men and the horses were trying to find shelter.

The almost incessant crashes of thunder were followed by lurid flashes of lightning that turned the darkness into dazzling light for a moment. After each flash the gloom seemed inkier than before.

Although Jim's and Buck's horses were restless, and trembled at each crash of thunder, they did not break away. Their heads were protected by the overhanging ledge, and neither of them, even though he had been free to run away, would have done so. Like Old Snorter, they were range horses with plenty of experience in such storms as this. But it was harder on the colt, Tiger. He had gone through a few of these wild storms but nothing like as many as his mother had. Besides, he was still very young and his skin was not as tough as hers; his nerves were more sensitive and so he was more aware of discomfort than she was. Still, he was a wild colt and had been pelted by rain before, so he took it as bravely as he could, though in previous storms Old Snorter had been able to run with him to a ravine filled with big trees which had kept the worst of the driving rain off him. Tiger trembled at the ear-splitting crashes of thunder and he was frightened by the blinding flashes of lightning. But he had complete faith in his mother, so he stayed close beside her and waited, snorting and blowing the water from his nostrils. Unlike a human being, he could not think of anything but the present. He could only stand against the bank and wait—for how long, he did not know.

Jim and Buck had seen Old Snorter and Tiger when they took to the cleft in the bank for shelter, but when the storm struck in full fury, they no longer made any attempt to look around the spur in the hill towards the mare and her colt. They kept back under the shelf of rock and stood there holding the reins of their horses. When the lightning flashed, giving them light to see by, they looked down on the draw below. It had been nearly dry when they first got here, but now it was quickly filling with running water, which was churned violently by the rain beating down upon it.

The storm had come down from the northwest, where, well up the stream, the heavens had recently opened in a sudden cloudburst. When this happened, sometimes a wall of water came rushing down the draw in a flash flood. Jim, who happened to look at the draw in the next flash of lightning, shouted in Buck's ear, " Look! Buck! A cloudburst! " Buck looked as the lightning flashed again, and saw the great wall of water sweeping down.

Instantly Jim and Buck became alarmed for the mare and the colt standing in the cleft against the high bank, only a little above the draw. The men did not see the water sweep them away, but they soon knew that was what had happened. A glare of lightning showed them Old Snorter and Tiger swimming valiantly in the flood not far from the shore, Tiger a little behind his mother.

After Old Snorter and Tiger had been carried a little way past the place where Jim and Buck stood, the men saw that both horses had made a landing. They had been carried into the opening of a cut that ran back from the draw towards the hill, and there they stood in quiet water which no more than covered their legs.

Jim and Buck did not see the mare and her colt get out of the flooded cut, but a little later in another lightning flash they saw them standing at the base of the hill. They had leaped on a pile of fallen earth and had splashed their way up out of the water.

When next it lightened, Old Snorter and Tiger could not be seen, but Jim and Buck guessed where they had taken shelter. That was where they saw them a few minutes later. Old Snorter and Tiger were huddling in a clump of cedars that grew in a cut near the foot of the hill.

The men decided to wait until the worst of the

storm had passed before they rode down after them. Then, if they found them still there, they would try to rope the colt.

Although these Western storms drove down with sudden violence, they often stopped almost as suddenly as they had begun. This was what happened now. Soon the rain abruptly ceased. After an extremely brief lull, hail came pelting down. The hailstones were not large, but when the cowboys' horses felt them peppering their hindquarters, they tried to crowd farther under the ledge. They did not, however, make any attempt to lunge away. Suddenly the hail stopped and all was calm.

Now, as the sky rapidly grew lighter, Jim and Buck were ready to act. With the coils of rope on their arms, they mounted, and rode down along the edge of the flooded draw. The air had grown chill and the horses wanted to gallop, but Jim and Buck held them to a prancing trot. Their black hoofs looked blacker than ever, washed clean by the dripping grass. The torrent beside them rushed swiftly on with a sullen, roaring sound. Such swift, rushing floods were dangerous for the best of swimmers, either man or horse.

The wooded cut in the hill formed a kind of trap for Old Snorter and her colt, but in the sudden danger from the surge of water, she had thought only of getting away from the flood. That was why she had run into this cut in the hill, which ended in a sheer bank about ten feet high, with slopes on both sides too steep to climb. If riders should suddenly appear at the entrance of the cut, she could run only in one direction— straight at them.

All at once Old Snorter saw the riders appear at the open end of the cut where she and her colt had taken refuge. She threw up her head, uttered a loud snort of defiance, and instantly came charging towards them, with Tiger running close behind.

Buck and Jim began whirling their ropes for the throw. Buck sent his rope flying for Old Snorter, but she was smart enough to duck her head low, and the rope missed. Because Buck's horse was in her way, Old Snorter, in her determination to escape, struck him with her broad chest, knocked him to his knees, and plunged on. But before she could check herself, she was right on the edge of the steep earth bank beside the draw. The earth of the bank gave way beneath her weight, and she fell into the angry torrent. She went down but came up swimming, her head showing above the dark, rushing water that carried her swiftly down the draw.

In the meantime, Jim had succeeded in casting his loop over Tiger's head. Tiger kept on running, but Jim did not want him to run too hard against the rope, so he increased the speed of his own horse and succeeded in jerking Tiger to a stand without throwing him. Instantly Tiger whirled around, which faced him towards Jim. All this, which happened very quickly, kept Jim so busy that he did not see what had happened to Old Snorter.

When Buck's horse got up on his feet, Buck saw Tiger, almost on his haunches, pulling back on the rope that held him. The loop on Tiger's neck was a slip noose. By pulling straight back with all his strength, he made the slip noose tighten, and it began to choke him. Wild with fear, he stopped pulling and stood still, with his feet well apart, to get his breath.

When Buck rode up, Jim handed him the rope. Then Jim dismounted and, holding his horse by the bridle reins, walked slowly up to Tiger, talking to him soothingly. Tiger was badly frightened. Never before in his brief life had a man come so near him. He was afraid of all men, because Old Snorter had taught him to be. He stood there, trembling with fear and the exertion of his desperate effort to get free.

Jim kept talking to Tiger softly. Tiger did not know that if he stepped forward and let the rope slacken, it would not grip his throat so hard. He had never had a chance to learn anything about a rope.

Jim continued to walk slowly up to Tiger. talking to him quietly all the while. " Hallo, little feller. It's too bad that rope choked you. Buck and I don't want to hurt you at all. Be quiet now, I'll fix you up."

As Jim walked nearer, Tiger threw his head up quickly. For a moment it seemed as if he were going to fight, but the pain of the choking rope controlled him.

Jim and Buck never forgot the little scene that followed, as Jim came even closer and put his hands on the frightened colt. Tiger quivered but he stood still. Jim began tying another rope on his neck so that it would hold but would not slip. Still trembling, Tiger did not move a hoof. He just stood there gasping for breath.

Jim said, " Now that's fine of you, Tiger. You're a little horse that's got sense. You're terribly scared, yet you don't go crazy. You've got sense, and a lot of it."

Jim's quiet manner helped the colt to stand still and receive the aid he needed so badly. Jim finished tying the new rope on Tiger's neck and then cut the slip noose of the first rope with his knife. Mounting his own horse, he took a turn of the end of the rope around his saddle horn. When Tiger found that he could breathe easily, he lunged back and fought to get free, but the rope held him.

Just then Jim and Buck heard a loud snort coming from a short distance down the flooded draw. They saw Old Snorter's head just above a bank in the draw where a backwater pool had formed. Old Snorter had saved herself from the raging torrent by swimming into the pool, but the bank rose so sharply that she could not leap out.

Buck said, " Well! Well! Look who's there! If

she doesn't try to plunge back into the stream, I'll throw my loop over her head and help her out."

Buck walked his horse down towards the backwater. As he drew nearer, Old Snorter uttered one loud snort after another, and they were snorts of unmistakable anger and defiance. As Buck rode still nearer, her eyes blazed and she snorted even louder. He thought she might turn and swim out into the flood, but she did not. She had no intention of leaving Tiger. Buck came up close, tossed his loop over her head, took a turn of the rope around his saddle horn, and slowly rode his horse away until the rope began to pull on the mare.

When Old Snorter felt the pull of the rope on her neck, she struggled quickly to the open ground above. The instant she saw Tiger, she neighed shrilly and started galloping towards him, with Buck riding after her. Tiger neighed in answer to his mother.

Buck galloped his horse towards the place where Tiger stood, because he did not want Old Snorter to run against the rope held by the saddle horn. Neither he nor Jim wanted to harm the old outlaw mare, whom they admired. She had not only won the freedom she longed for, she had known how to keep it. They wanted to lead her and Tiger peacefully, and they tried to.

When the mare got close to Tiger, Buck pulled his horse up so that the rope was almost tight on her neck. Jim, on the other side, held Tiger by the long rope. Old Snorter put her nose against Tiger and talked to him in her own way by making little anxious whinnying sounds. Tiger's eyes were wide and he breathed rapidly in his fright even while he received his mother's greetings.

Buck called out, " Jim, she's trying to tell the little feller what a mess they're both in! "

" Yes," Jim called back, " and she's likely telling him she'll break loose and maybe get him loose too."

Jim had no more than spoken when Old Snorter whirled and looked at him. She held her head up, her eyes blazed, and she snorted with defiance. Then, before Buck could do anything except stare at her, she came thundering past him at a gallop. Old Snorter knew all about what a rope could do, but she was desperate. She rushed by at such a speed that Buck barely had time to wheel his horse in the same direction that she was taking. Buck had full confidence in his well-trained horse. With the rope around the saddle horn, he pulled sharply on the bridle reins, and his horse sat back on his haunches. Old Snorter hit the end of the rope and was thrown to the ground, but now an unusual thing happened: the rope broke at the saddle horn. Generally a cowboy's rope does not break, but Old Snorter was big and heavy. She jumped up at once and dashed away, with the long rope trailing behind her.

Jim and Buck watched the old mare. She ran only a little way before she stopped, looked back, and snorted loudly. Then she turned and leaped up to the top of the hill, where she stood and looked down. Perhaps she knew enough to realise that her colt would be led up the hill in her direction, because this was the nearest way to the ranch.

Jim, leading Tiger, started his horse up the hill at an angle, with Buck riding close behind Tiger. This made Tiger leap up the hill and Buck, at the back of him, kept urging his horse on, in order to keep Tiger going.

Standing waiting on the hilltop, Old Snorter nickered shrilly to the colt. Encouraged by the sound, he plunged up rapidly to join her. Soon he reached the summit and stood there close beside his mother, as if he were sure that she could help him get free.

Buck started his horse forward slowly, hoping he might get near enough to pick up the end of the long rope that trailed from Old Snorter's neck. But she was too cunning for that. She went trotting away, her head and tail high. When she reached a safe distance she whirled, faced Buck and Jim, and emitted such snorts that Jim said, " Buck, I don't reckon we ever had a horse that could snort as loud as that old mare."

" We never did," said Buck. " You'd think it would strain her, yet she's plumb healthy."

Old Snorter and Tiger stood there on the hilltop, their rain-washed coats looking even more black than usual. Tiger, still scared, was trembling. Old Snorter had her head up in defiance, but deep within her there was a feeling of disappointment and trouble, because she knew she was helpless to free her colt from the hands of these hated men.

Buck said, " Well, Jim, we might as well start for home with Tiger. I wish that rope was off Old Snorter's neck. Unless we get hold of it, she might get tangled up somewhere and never get loose. But

I don't think that will happen. I think she'll keep close to us all the way."

When they started on, with Jim leading Tiger, Old Snorter quickly galloped ahead of them. For quite a distance their way led across a broad, level high land. Tiger kept moving at a steady prancing trot when he realised that the rope still held him. Buck rode close behind.

The sun was shining and there was a delightful, cool freshness in the air, after the rain. The broad, open land was dotted here and there with small clumps of trees, whose leaves glowed vividly green.

CHAPTER TWO

IN OUTLAW HANDS

Jim and Buck rode steadily on across the high land in the direction of the ranch-house. Buck rode behind Jim. When Tiger stopped, as he did from time to time, Buck rode up and tapped him with the end of his rope. Then Tiger leaped forward until Jim's lead rope checked him. The colt went along this way for quite a while, but at last he settled down to a quiet trot, fairly close to Jim's horse. This pleased the men very much.

It was getting late. The sun had already set, and Jim and Buck knew that night would be upon them before they reached the ranch-house, so they decided to see if they could get Tiger to gallop for a while. Jim put his horse into a fast trot. At the same time, Buck tapped Tiger with the end of his rope, and the colt sprang forward in a gallop. To keep up with him, Jim had to urge his horse into a faster and faster pace. Tiger acted as though he thought he might escape by running with this desperate speed. As he raced along in full flight, he gave a long, shrill nicker that carried far over the darkening plain. Old Snorter, who was dashing on ahead of them and at one side, answered him at once. Buck and Jim could see that as she galloped her head was jerked down now and then, when she stepped on the long, trailing rope. Sometimes the force of the jerk almost stopped her in her tracks.

Jim thought Tiger was setting too fast a pace for himself, so he slowed his horse down and pulled Tiger to a stop. The colt was breathing fast and was excited, so Jim held his horse to a walk, hoping that Tiger would quieten down.

As night fell, stars began to glitter in the sky, except where a long cloud on the northern horizon stretched upward. But the cloud did not move, and Buck and Jim knew that it was not likely they would get any rain from it.

Jim held his horse at a steady jog trot, but Tiger kept going into a dancing trot and then into a gallop until he was checked by the backward pull of the rope.

Now they were travelling over a stretch of wild,

rolling land, cut here and there by deep tree-filled gorges. The tops of the trees in the ravines loomed dark against the grassland beside them. Soon they rode along the edge of one of the largest of these ravines, known as Sheridan Gorge. They knew that the head of this ravine reached far back in the high land towards the ranch house. The moon slipped above the eastern horizon and, as it rose, lighted up the whole countryside for the travellers.

Tiger was now so apprehensive and ill at ease that he could not take things calmly. He could not keep to a steady pace; he would trot for a while and then once more would try to gallop, only to be pulled back by the rope on his neck.

Jim and Buck had been paying little attention to Old Snorter, for she had been galloping along some distance away, occasionally snorting loudly. But all of a sudden she made a surprise move. Nickering loudly, she rushed up so close to Tiger that she could almost have touched him. Then she leaped away at a run, nickering shrilly as if she were trying to tell him to follow her. She ran a short distance, stopped, whirled, and came back. Again she passed Tiger so close that her side almost brushed his. On each of her dashes Old

Snorter passed on the side next to the deep gorge. Now she came plunging back once more, straight towards the colt. Buck's rope trailed from her neck but the cowboy made no attempt to catch her. It would be difficult in the darkness, and the important thing was to get Tiger back to the ranch.

Tiger, excited by having his mother so near him, began to leap up on his hind legs and fight to get free. In disgust, Buck decided to drive the old mare away. As she came running back again, he spurred his horse to meet her, his quirt held high, ready to strike. Buck's horse jumped forward swiftly at the touch of the spurs and Old Snorter was caught by surprise. She leaped away to avoid Buck, getting so close to the steep bank of the ravine that she lost her balance and went rolling down the side through the thick growth of bushes.

Jim stopped his horse and held Tiger, while Buck quickly dismounted. In the moonlight he could see the big mare go crashing through the bushes and finally land at the bottom of the gorge in a wild tangle of briers and vines. Buck and Jim did not want her to be injured, so they were both glad when they heard her snort from the depths of the ravine. Buck looked down for a minute, but he could not distinguish the black mare in the tangled growth. He heard her blow through her nostrils once or twice and decided she had not been hurt. Tiger had quieted down. He stood with his head up, looking towards Buck and the place where Old Snorter had disappeared. He blew through his nose and watched, as if he were waiting for her to return.

Buck continued to listen, and when he heard Old Snorter thrashing around in the vines and thickets, he was sure she was on her feet. " Jim," he said, " I don't think she's hurt. The bushes broke her fall. I can hear her moving around in the brush down there, but with that rope trailing from her neck she's likely to get caught on something and maybe starve unless she can break the rope."

While Buck stood at the edge of the ravine looking down into its depths, they heard Old Snorter give a shrill nicker to her colt. At the sound Tiger stood still and answered with his own loud nicker. Jim said, " Buck, he's saying to her, ' Here I am, but they've got me. I can't get loose.' "

Buck mounted his horse and they started on

their way again. Tiger was more uneasy now, for he knew something had happened to his mother. He ran forward against the rope until it brought him up short, and then he turned and tried to run back, but Buck rode over to him and tapped him with the quirt.

Old Snorter could still be heard nickering in the depths of the gorge, but gradually the sounds grew fainter and faded in the distance. Buck decided that the rope on the mare's neck had already been caught in the bushes, for otherwise she would be following along in the gorge in order to stay as near her colt as possible.

The distant cloud blotted out some of the stars, but many stars still gleamed and the rising moon gave even more light now. It was bright enough for Jim and Buck to see that they were approaching a drop in the land where some thick bushes grew.

Tiger was running ahead as far as his rope would let him. He had almost reached one of the clumps of bushes when two grey wolves leaped out from the undergrowth and ran like slinking shadows across the open land towards the deep gorge a short distance away. Tiger stopped quickly and snorted in fear. The wolves disappeared under the dark, low-hanging branches of the trees at the edge of the ravine.

Buck said, " Jim, those were a couple of big ones. If Old Snorter is caught by her rope down there, they may tackle her."

" If they do," said Jim, " they'll have a fight on their hands."

" That's so," said Buck. " If only the two of them tackle her, she'll make buzzard bait out of them."

Tiger was nickering loudly, but no answering sound came from the gorge. It was impossible to find out what had happened to Old Snorter, so Jim and Buck kept Tiger moving ahead in the moonlight night towards the ranch-house and the stables.

In the meantime, Old Snorter was in trouble, but not because of the dangling rope. Horse thieves had come into this territory, knowing that many range horses were rounded up for branding on the Sheridan ranch each spring. A band of six rustlers were out on this particular night, looking for horses on Sheridan's range. They had heard the shrill nickers of Old Snorter and had found a place where they could ride down into the ravine.

When they reached the bottom of the gorge, they all dismounted. One of them stole back up to the top on foot and peeped out from the shadowy cover of the low-hanging branches along the edge. He heard a loud nicker and then saw two riders moving along near the ravine with a black colt. He watched briefly and then crept down to his confederates and told them what he had seen. The instant they heard that riders from the ranch were close by, each man held his hand over the nose of his horse so that it could not nicker and betray them to the two riders above. They knew that the men on the Sheridan range were all experienced and extremely alert.

All the horse thieves could plainly hear the shrill nickering of Tiger as the two riders passed along the open land not far from the gorge. But sounds came again from farther down the ravine, and they realised that the stray horse they had heard before was moving towards them.

It was difficult for the thieves to keep their own mounts quiet. They were restless, but the men killfully managed to hold them and to keep a hand clamped on the nose of each horse.

The horses were nervous at being held this way and they kept tossing their heads up, trying to jerk their noses free. One horse started to back towards a clump of bushes, but the nearest man saw the movement and kicked him in the flank so that he jumped forward and stood still. The outlaws knew that these horses, which they had stolen on nearby ranges, had been missed and that all the range riders were alerted for rustlers; so it was absolutely necessary not to let them make a sound.

Suddenly the horses began to plunge about so violently that they could hardly be held. Old Snorter was crashing through the bushes towards them, and the sounds made by the big black mare made all the other horses jump.

The thieves were afraid that the cowboys had heard the commotion, so one of them climbed up the side of the ravine to look out over the moonlit plain. The two horsemen with the small colt had made good time and were now only faintly visible in the distance. When the scout came back and reported that there was no longer any danger, the men decided to try and catch the horse in the ravine near them.

Old Snorter was only a short distance away, but the trees and bushes hid the men and their horses, so she did not realise they were near. The mare thrashed through the bushes, nickered, and then leaped along the gorge, bursting into the open space where the men stood with their horses. Old Snorter checked her speed, but then leaped forward to pass them, for in spite of this new danger she wanted to follow her colt. As she tried to pass, one of the men saw the trailing rope and grabbed it just as the mare was halted momentarily by a thicket of tall brush and vines. The man took a quick half hitch of the rope around a tree.

Old Snorter plunged on, and then was almost thrown by the hard jerk on the rope on her neck. She whirled about to face her new enemies. She blew through her nostrils loudly, frightened and desperate, but ready to seize any chance for escape.

Two of the men slowly approached the big mare with ropes in their hands. As they neared her she leaped aside, but one man managed to cast his loop over her head, and then the other man im-

mediately roped her too. Old Snorter had the sense
to know she could struggle no longer. She had
long ago had experience with ropes, and she knew
when to stand still.

The men worked quickly, putting two new
ropes on her neck that would not slip and choke
her, and taking off the other ropes. Two other
men rode up, one on either side of the mare, ready
to lead her out of the gorge and up to the open
land. After riding a short distance along the gorge,
they found a place that sloped less steeply, where
Old Snorter could be led up to the top. The two
men with Old Snorter went first, and the others
followed on their horses. Even at this spot the
ravine side was so steep that the horses had to
plunge and leap to make the climb. Whenever Old
Snorter balked, the man riding behind her struck
her on the rump with his quirt. At each blow she
leaped forward, and finally the men reached the
open ground with their captive.

When Old Snorter got to the top, she sent forth
a loud, shrill nicker for Tiger. The men were
alarmed at the noise and immediately set out at
a fast pace in the opposite direction from that
taken by the two riders with the colt. Old Snorter

had no chance to escape, for each of the two men riding beside her still had one end of his rope tied on her neck and the other fastened securely around his saddle horn. She tried to stop once, but one of the men riding close behind struck her sharply with his short whip.

She was forced to gallop with them this way for miles, and despite her great endurance she began to tire. Old Snorter suffered from the fast pace and also from the anxiety of losing her colt. She began to breathe more rapidly and the sweat came out on her coat, but still she galloped on. However, the hard treatment and the loss of her freedom did not make her forget her missing colt. Since her first attempt to call Tiger had been punished by the quirt, she knew that she would be hurt if she tried to call again and that there was nothing to do but wait for an opportunity to escape.

At last the rustlers pulled their horses to a stop in a low-lying valley dotted with scattered trees. The big cloud in the east had grown no bigger and the moon and stars illuminated all the valley. The men dismounted, hobbled their horses, and turned them loose to graze.

Old Snorter was tied to a tree with a long rope so that she could graze too, but by this time she was too nervous to eat. A man had been stationed near her ready to use his whip if she nickered. She stood with her head up, looking back towards the gorge where so much had happened. Tiger had been taken from her there, and she longed to run back in that direction. The guard saw her lift her head high as if she were about to nicker, and he sprang towards her, threatening her with his whip. Old Snorter did not nicker. She only made a low sound like a groan, and lowered her head until it almost reached the ground. She remained quietly in this position, having lost all interest in everything around her.

Her guard, having decided that she would make no more trouble, joined the others to discuss what they should do with the mare. They all saw that they had captured a magnificent horse, and each one hoped to own her, so they decided to draw lots for her. One of the men hid some little sticks in his hand, leaving only the top ends in sight. It was agreed that the man who got the shortest stick would own Old Snorter. The drawing was over in a few minutes, and a short, thin fellow with a black moustache had drawn the short stick.

The men had planned to rest and let the horses graze here only for a short time, since they wanted to cover as much distance as possible that night. As they were preparing to leave, the man who had won Old Snorter said that he would ride her and lead his other horse. " She may be a quite a bucker," he said, " but she's so tired I can soon tame her down."

All the rustlers gathered in a group to see him ride the big black mare. He got his saddle and dropped it on Old Snorter's back. She flinched when she felt the weight, but she made no move. Her new owner drew the saddle cinch up tight on her, put the bridle on without difficulty, and then prepared to mount. He wore, as they all did, big wheel spurs with sharp cutting edges.

Old Snorter had not been ridden since her days at the Sheridan ranch, and then she had been known as one of the worst bucking horses in the outfit. She had thrown so many of the best riders that they always mounted her in a corral, and each morning the same thing happened. After she had thrown two or three men she became too tired to uck, and then anyone could ride her that day and she was, strangely enough, an excellent cattle horse. But the next morning she bucked just as hard as ever. John Sheridan had kept her only because she was such a beautiful mare and because he hoped that in time she would be tamed. But she never stopped bucking and she never lost the desire to run free in the wild range country. Ten years had not changed her, and her longing for freedom was just as strong as ever. In spite of Old Snorter's hatred of being ridden, she had never attacked a man, because she had never been treated unkindly. John Sheridan had not allowed his men to wear spurs when they rode her, and they had never struck her with a whip.

Now the mare stood still with her head up and her eyes on the man near her. She was ready to fight as soon as he swung up in the saddle on her back. The horse thief put his foot in the stirrup and mounted quickly. Old Snorter immediately began bucking hard, and at once he tried the usual ways of breaking a bucking horse. He whipped her with the stinging quirt and gouged her sensitive flanks with his cruel spurs. Old Snorter, driven wild with pain, bucked as she had never done before. Somehow, her new owner managed to stay on, and the more she fought the harder he gouged her sides with his spurs.

If the mare had been fresh and rested, as she always had been on those early mornings at the Sheridan ranch, she would have thrown her rider in a short time. But she was desperately tired now after her efforts to free Tiger from his captors and the long gallop with the band of rustlers. A sudden surge of strength came to her, however, in spite of her exhaustion, and she reared up suddenly on her hind legs, whirling so quickly that when she came down her rider lost his balance and was thrown to the ground. Driven into a frenzy by her pain, Old Snorter rushed at him and struck him with her powerful front hoof. Then she charged at the other men, her ears back, her mouth open, and her teeth gleaming faintly in the dark. They scattered and ran like rabbits, but Old Snorter reached one man and knocked him down just before he gained the protection of a clump of brush.

When she whirled to look for the others, she saw that none of them were near her. Now she was free to escape, and she leaped away with all

he speed left in her. Instinctively, she ran towards
the place where she had last seen Tiger. The bridle
and saddle were still on her, but fortunately the
bridle reins had been tied together so that they
lay on top of her neck and did not drag on the
ground.

Hours later, Jim and Buck were approaching
the ranch with Tiger. Clouds had overspread all
the sky and the night was pitch dark. Suddenly
they heard the shrill nicker of a horse close behind
them, and Old Snorter thundered past so close
that she almost brushed against Tiger.

Jim had taken a half turn of the lead rope on
his saddle horn. If the colt started to plunge, Jim
knew that he could quickly take another turn in
order to hold him. But he had also given Tiger a
little more rope than usual, so that as he danced
about he would not feel a constant pull on his
neck. He had wanted to be kind to the small colt,
so frightened and lonely at being separated from
his mother, but now he suddenly regretted his
kindness.

As Old Snorter shot past, Tiger leaped high on

his hind legs and jerked the rope off the saddle horn. Before Jim could make a move, the colt was free and running as fast as he could to keep up with his mother. The long rope was still tied around his neck and trailed on the ground behind him. It all happened so quickly that Jim could only sit and watch in amazement as Tiger and the rope disappeared.

Jim and Buck galloped their horses, following the sounds of Old Snorter's hoofs on the sod. There was no other noise and the night was so black that they could see nothing. Old Snorter and Tiger ran close together and took full advantage of the cover the darkness gave them.

The two men heard the mare's hoofbeats off to the left, and they turned in that direction, but it was impossible to get near the runaways. They soon gave up, deciding they might have a better chance of recapturing Tiger the next day.

As they rode back towards the ranch, Jim said, " With that long rope trailing from Tiger's neck. he's likely to get caught on something."

" That's so," Buck answered, " and if he gets caught that way, we'll have to find him soon or e'll starve. Old Snorter will keep near him if his rope gets caught, and she'll help him if wolves try to get him. She can take care of them, but she can't keep him from starving. We'll have to start out at daylight and hunt for him."

CHAPTER THREE

TIGER IS FOUND AGAIN

FOUR DAYS later Jim Summers and Buck Davis were still trying to find Tiger and his mother. Jim was worried about the dangerous rope that was trailing from the colt's neck when he escaped. Since that night, none of the men on John Sheridan's ranch had seen either Black Tiger or Old Snorter.

Late in the afternoon of the fourth day, Jim was riding alone in one of the wildest regions of the vast, lonely range—a valley dotted with tall pines and cedar trees, between two high, steep hills. On the hillside at his left, Jim could see several rocky ledges that jutted out. A grove of towering pines at the right kept Jim from seeing what was on that side. He rode along the edge of the grove, holding his horse to a walk and looking sharply at the ground ahead for even the smallest sign of Tiger nd Old Snorter. The horse, a big bay, seemed to understand what was going on. He walked with his head up and his ears cocked forward. He was alert, like most ranch horses. He had learned that he might have to move, and move quickly, at any moment.

Suddenly Jim pulled his horse to a stop and jerked his rifle from the holster on the saddle in front of him. As he came to the end of the pine grove, he had seen the head of a mountain lion which was crouching on a ledge of rock near the foot of the hill at his right. At the same instant Jim also saw Tiger, standing very close to a tree near the ledge. Jim felt certain that Tiger's rope had caught there and that the colt, trying vainly to get free, had walked around and around the tree until at last he was held with his head close against the trunk itself.

Knowing that the mountain lion could easily destroy Tiger, Jim quickly dismounted and, holding the reins of his horse in the crook of one arm, raised his rifle. Just then Old Snorter appeared from behind a clump of trees farther away. Jim was sure she was not aware of Tiger's danger, but even if she had been, she was too far away to help.

The big mountain cat lifted its head a little, as if preparing to spring. Then the rifle shot rang out, shattering the stillness of the lonely mountain valley. The lion plunged from the ledge and lay motionless on the ground below. Jim quickly rode over to make sure that it was dead, and then rode back to Tiger.

When Old Snorter heard the rifle shot and saw the mountain lion tumble down from the ledge, she rushed towards Tiger, snorting wildly. Her snorts became even louder when she saw Jim ride up to her son.

" Well, Tiger," Jim said, as he approached the frightened colt, " even if that mountain cat hadn't got you, you would soon have been plumb dead anyway. A little feller like you all wound up on this tree, starving for water and grass, couldn't take it much longer."

Jim could see from Tiger's condition that he had been helpless here for several days. He was fearfully thin, and the look in his eyes showed his suffering. Water was what he needed most. When Jim came close, Tiger at first tried to pull away. He was afraid of this man, but he was held tight by the rope and was too weak to struggle. His sides, eeply sunken from lack of food and water, moved in and out rapidly as he panted with fear.

Jim rode his horse to a nearby tree and tied him. He took a coil of rope and walked slowly over to Tiger. Talking soothingly, he put one hand gently on Tiger's neck. At first Tiger flinched at the touch and stood rigid, but Jim rubbed him a little and soon he allowed Jim to work on the rope that was pulling him so close to the tree.

While Jim was busy with Tiger, Old Snorter stood at a distance, blowing through her nose to make it plain that she did not want Jim to touch her colt. He paid no attention to her, but kept on working until he had Tiger free from the tree. Then he carefully tied his own rope around Tiger's neck in such a way that it could not hurt him, but firmly enough so that he would not be able to get away again. He took a good look at Old Snorter and, to his surprise, saw that she was wearing a saddle and bridle. The bridle reins were broken and the loose ends hung down.

When Tiger felt himself free from the tree at last, he did not try to run away. Instead, he merely stepped back a little, and looked at Jim. Although his eyes showed fear, it was not as intense as if he had been caught while free and in possession of all his strength.

The first thing Jim wanted to do was to get Tiger to the nearest water. He looked towards Old Snorter, who had moved away and now stood on the other side of a rise in the ground. Jim started in her direction, thinking she might lead him to a pool of water.

When Jim pulled on the rope, Tiger held back a little, but he was too weak to resist much. Besides, he was beginning to understand that Jim, the first human being to touch him, had not hurt him. This man who now urged him to come along had helped him out of a bad situation. The gentle, quiet tone of the man's voice reassured Tiger, and he started to walk forward slowly behind him.

Jim's notion about the location of water proved to be correct, for there was a small pool where he had seen Old Snorter standing. As Jim came nearer with her colt, she blew a loud snort and galloped off. A short distance away she stopped and turned to watch.

When Tiger saw the water he plunged forward to reach it quickly, only to fall to his knees. For a moment he rested on the ground, while Jim stood beside him and talked to him quietly. Then Tiger struggled to his feet and, once at the pool, thrust his nose down to the water and began to drink.

Jim knew the danger of letting a horse in Tiger's condition drink too much or too quickly. Such a mistake could cost a horse his life. However, it is not easy to get a horse away from the water under such circumstances, and Jim had to pull Tiger back sharply when he had had as much water as he could safely drink. Tiger struggled to stay in the pool but, because of his weakness, he was not able to resist. Away from the water at last, he stood breathing hard from his exertion.

" Now I'll let you eat grass awhile," Jim said, " and then you can have some more water."

As Jim and the colt started towards a patch of rich grass, Jim saw that Tiger did not like the feel of the rope tied around his neck. He was not used to it and he was afraid. Jim walked up to him and said, " Don't be scared, Tiger. I won't hurt you." He rubbed Tiger's neck and repeated, " Come on, let's get to the grass."

This time Tiger seemed more willing, and he allowed himself to be led towards the grass. As they got nearer to it, Tiger lunged towards it wildly, so that Jim had to hurry to keep up with him. As soon as he reached the grass, he plunged his nose down into it and began biting off big mouthfuls hungrily.

All this time Old Snorter had been standing on a small hill not far from her colt, watching what was going on. Now she snorted louder than ever and began galloping around in a circle. She would stop suddenly and then start off again, racing around or dashing away, snorting all the time. She hoped Tiger would follow her on one of her dashes, and when he did not, she galloped back to within ten feet of Jim and Tiger, stopped short, and stood there.

" Say, old lady," Jim said, " do you mean to tackle me? I'll show you! " He threw his rope so that the loose end lay about fifteen feet behind him on the ground. Then he jerked it skilfully, making it shoot out from behind him and snap Old Snorter sharply on the shoulder. She leaped back in surprise, her eyes blazing, but did not run away. Jim looked at her. " You stay where you are," he said. " Tiger is hungry. I'll take care of him and I won't hurt him."

Jim watched as Tiger took one huge mouthful

of grass after another. His gaze strayed to Old Snorter and then across the valley. Coming from the west was a man on a long-legged sorrel that Jim knew was Buck's horse. Jim smiled in great satisfaction.

Buck rode up and dismounted. " Well, Jim, how on earth did you get him? " he asked. Then he took a closer look at Tiger. " I think I know by the looks of him. He was caught by that rope."

Jim described what had happened, and told about the stalking lion. " There it is," he said, and pointed to the great form of the tawny-coloured beast stretched on the ground.

Buck looked at it and then at Tiger, who was still eagerly devouring the grass. " You got here just in time," he said. " An hour later and you'd have found a dead colt. With lots of grass and water, Tiger will soon be as good as new. Say, Jim," he added, " it's miles to the ranch-house. I think we'd better start along after he's had a little more to eat."

" I think so too," said Jim. " We'll go slow and stop now and then to let him graze. I'm mighty pleased you're here, Buck. We can take care of Tiger better. And Old Snorter may try to make trouble. How do you suppose she got that saddle and bridle?"

"My guess is that horse thieves caught her somehow," Buck said. "One of them managed to get on her. She did the rest and got away."

"I think so too," Jim said.

Buck looked serious. "I'm glad I'm going with you," he said. "I saw those horse thieves this morning over by Antelope Springs. I had been riding with Bud Maxwell, but we separated and I was alone when I saw them. I rode up on a ridge quite a way from the Springs, and I had no more than showed up when the three of them put spurs to their horses and rode off. They disappeared in no time."

Jim frowned. "Well," he said, "it's late and we'll have to travel with Tiger in the dark to-night. But the moon will be shining, and I don't think the horse thieves will bother us on the way. They aim to keep a good distance from us fellers when they do their stealing."

"That's so," said Buck. "We can keep to the high land and take our time. But that outfit sure has been a pest to the range men. Seems as if they're like three wolves."

"Yes," said Jim, "they sure are as cunning as wolves. Bud Maxwell said he heard they stole three of the best horses over on the Lone Star ranch last week."

While Jim and Buck were talking, Tiger was eating grass as fast as he could. It was remarkable how he already seemed to have lost most of his fear. The quiet way the men spoke to him and the kind treatment they gave him had made him feel they were his friends. When Jim led him to the pool again to let him drink, Tiger, of his own accord, walked close behind him.

As the sun sank behind the high hill in the west, Buck and Jim talked quietly to each other about Tiger and watched him graze. The men were pleased to see that he was quieter now. A good horse means a lot to ranchers, and to these men a colt seemed almost the same as a small child does to people in settled country. Buck and Jim planned to take good care of this one.

Old Snorter seemed to have accepted the situation. She was grazing some distance away, apparently paying little attention to Tiger now that he was more at ease.

Before they started out for the ranch-house,

Jim and Buck let their horses drink at the pool, and then they gave Tiger a final drink too. By this time the stars were shining in the clear sky and the air was cool. Tiger pulled back only once, when he felt the rope pull on his neck, but after that he made no trouble.

Jim and Buck took the easiest way back to the ranch. So as not to tire the colt unnecessarily, they kept in the valley until they found a spot where the hill sloped gradually upwards, and then they rode up the hillside at an angle. On the way up they stopped several times to let Tiger rest, each time waiting until he started again of his own accord. Whenever Tiger stopped, Jim instantly stopped his own horse. At last they reached the broad high land. There Jim and Buck dismounted and talked softly to Tiger, telling him what a " fine little feller " he was.

The high land was uneven, full of small rises and dips that sometimes made it impossible to see very far ahead or behind. But every now and then the men could see Old Snorter following them at a distance. " That old mare isn't going to lose track of her colt," Buck said.

As they rode slowly across the highland in the

clear night, Jim and Buck kept up a steady stream of talk, mostly about the horse thieves, three of whom Buck had seen earlier that evening. Although none of the range men had ever seen more than three at one time, everyone felt certain that there were more. In those days of the old West, bands of horse thieves were common. They were a big problem to the ranch owners, because they had been known to steal as many as twenty-five or thirty horses at a time. They would drive these horses to some designated point, and there other dishonest men would buy them and ship them away in stock cars before they could be identified. That meant a serious loss for the ranch owner.

Jim and Buck held their horses to a slow walk, knowing that Tiger was not strong enough yet to move fast. When Tiger stopped and began to graze, Jim and Buck checked their horses and waited until he had eaten all he wanted. Then they all moved on again. Stopping now and then to let Tiger have a few mouthfuls of grass, and once to let him drink at a small pool, they travelled on until about one o'clock in the morning.

All at once Buck said, " Jim, I smell smoke. It seems to be ahead of us."

Sniffing the air, Jim too smelled smoke. " Maybe the horse thieves are sleeping in that dip in the land up ahead," he said softly, " and the smoke is from their camp fire."

" We'll soon find out," Buck said.

Jim's first thought was of Tiger. If the horse thieves had seen him at all when he was running, wild with Old Snorter, they must have tried to catch him. He was such a fine colt that they must have known he would bring a good price. Jim figured that they would surely try to get him again if ever they caught a glimpse of him. Although both he and Buck were armed with rifles, and each had a Colt .45 in his belt, he knew that two men unexpectedly coming upon a large band of horse thieves at night would be at great disadvantage.

Speaking in whispers, Jim and Buck discussed the situation and decided that they would investigate the smoke. Their alert horses had smelled it too, although it was carried only faintly on a very gentle breeze, and they walked slowly with their ears pricked up. The moonlight was so bright now that Buck and Jim could clearly see that the plain dropped down just ahead of them. Two scrub pines, surrounded by a number of bushes, grew near the slope, and Buck and Jim tied their own horses and Tiger to these trees. Stealing forward on foot, they came to a steep drop of about six feet, and now they could see a vast stretch of land spread out below. The moonlight revealed a sight there that made them tingle with excitement.

At least a dozen men were lying on the ground near a small fire, which shone only now and then as a dying ember blazed up and then died out. Beyond the place where the men slept, Jim and Buck could see horses grazing. Surely these were the horse thieves!

If there had been light enough to be sure that all the men were asleep, Jim and Buck would have tried to capture the thieves before they could make a move towards their guns. But these were desperate men, and almost certainly they would have posted two or three guards who would be awake and watching. Jim and Buck decided that the safest course would be to go around the place and get to the ranch with Tiger. As quickly and as quietly as they could, they stole back to the pines where they had left the horses, and in a few moments they were on their way towards the ranch-house again, this time making a wide detour around the thieves' encampment.

" Well, that was a close one," Jim said, when they were safely out of hearing distance of the thieves.

" It sure was," Buck agreed. " At least now we know about how many men and horses there are in that bunch."

All at once Old Snorter appeared. She was trotting at a fast clip, but she slowed down enough to keep abreast of Buck and Jim and the horses for a few minutes. Then she put on a burst of speed and rushed ahead towards the ranch. She almost seemed to know that her son was being taken to the same place where she had once lived for so many months.

Seeing Old Snorter again made Tiger restless and nervous. Here was his mother running near him, as free as he had been when he was with her, while he was being held in restraint by this creature on another horse. But he was less afraid of the men than he had been before he was rescued, and he knew that Jim had been kind to him.

CHAPTER FOUR

A WILLING PRISONER

OLD SNORTER stayed in the lead for another five minutes or so, and it seemed to Buck and Jim that she actually wanted to go back to the ranch corrals again and stay there with Tiger. But when she whirled around and galloped back towards her colt, her eyes blazing wildly, it was clear that she had not given up so easily. She rushed past Tiger, stopped, and nickered shrilly to him, as if to say, " Come, run with me! Break loose! " Then seeing that he scarcely turned his head to look at her, she raced out in front of him and tried to call him once more. Tiger was too tired to respond. He trotted steadily forward, paying almost no attention to her.

As Buck and Jim rode along with Tiger, Old Snorter kept running around them, her head up, her tail held high, while she blew out such loud snorts that Buck said, " Jim, I don't reckon

anyone ever heard another horse that could snort
like that old mare."

"It's because she's got such good lungs," Jim
answered. "That must be why we never could
catch her. I hope this little feller of hers proves to
have as good wind as she has."

Jim and Buck still believed Old Snorter would
go all the way to the ranch-house with Tiger. They
figured that she wanted to stick with her colt no
matter what, and if she could not get him to go
off with her, she would go wherever he went.
Tiger was still too weak to try to break loose and
run away with his mother, and he seemed almost
willing to go along with the men. But when the
mare ran close to him, he began to watch her in
a way that showed he might act differently when
he felt stronger.

Jim and Buck stopped now and then, when they
came to a pool of water, to let Tiger drink. After
they had travelled quite a distance they let him stop
and eat grass, and when they started on, Tiger
seemed more alert. The next time Old Snorter
rushed past, he broke into a trot, and Jim had to
put his own horse at a trot too, to let Tiger have
his way.

At last, just at sunrise, they could see the ranch house in the distance, with its stables and corrals at the foot of a slope covered with tall pine trees. Jim and Buck were relieved that the long trip was almost over.

Old Snorter's manner suddenly changed when she saw they were approaching the place she had run away from years before. Exactly what was in her mind no man could know, but Jim and Buck could see in her actions some evidence of her feelings. She grew quiet, and slowed down until Tiger came abreast of her. Then she walked beside him, touched his shoulder with her nose, and made soft sounds that Jim thought were meant to encourage him. But now she no longer held her head high as she walked beside her colt.

Buck, seeing all this, said, " Jim, I believe that old mare feels plumb bogged down."

" She sure acts like it," said Jim. " She looks as if she's just about given up."

Some of the men were in the ranch yard and they recognised Jim and Buck bringing Tiger in. They called to the others in the house and they all came outside to watch. John Sheridan said, " I wonder how that saddle got on the old mare. They

C

have no rope on her, yet she's coming along quie
She just won't leave the little feller. I always liked
that old mare, even when we ran our horses down
trying to catch her."

Old Snorter came into the yard and stood
quietly while some of the men put their hands on
her and talked to her. On looking at the wounds
in her sides and at the saddle, John Sheridan
decided, just as Jim and Buck had done, that horse
thieves had somehow got a rope on her and tried
to ride her.

Jim led Tiger into a stable and called to Old
Snorter, while all the men stood back and watched
to see what she would do. The mare walked up
to the open stable door and looked in at Jim, who
stood there holding Tiger. She then turned and
looked back at the men who were standing still,
making no move towards her. After that she
uttered a friendly sound to Tiger, walked into the
stable, and put her nose on him.

Jim called to the men, " Better shut the door.
I'm going to turn Tiger loose in here."

Promptly one of the men shut the door. Jim
took the rope from Tiger's neck and patted him.
Then he took a stout halter from a peg at the rear

of the stable, walked slowly up to Old Snorter, and talked to her quietly while he took off her bridle and saddle. After putting the halter on her head, he tied her to the manger, leaving Tiger free. Jim put some oats in a feed box for Old Snorter and also some in another box for Tiger, in case he was ready to eat oats. This did not seem likely, for a horse that has grown up in the wilds usually has to learn that oats and corn are good to eat. Now, however, Tiger was so hungry that he at once began to eat the oats.

The day passed and the night came on with a cloudy sky. Tiger and Old Snorter stood quietly in the darkness of the stable and stared at their new surroundings. When Jim came in, he was pleased to see that Tiger had eaten his oats and he put a fresh supply in both feed boxes. As soon as Jim had gone out, the mare began to eat her oats. Tiger, hearing her munching sounds, moved up close and put his nose out to smell what was in his own feed box. He remembered this smell. It was food he had found good before, so he ate up the oats and then began to walk about in the dark stable. As his nose touched the rear wall, he jerked his head back quickly. He walked slowly about in his prison, now and then cautiously touching his nose to one of the walls. Having found that he was enclosed by a barrier on all sides, he moved along the manger, smelling it, until he came back to his feed box. He licked the bottom of the box a few times. Then he stood beside his mother, staring into the darkness.

After some time had passed, the wind came up and made a steady sighing sound through the tall pines outside. Tiger could hear the wind blowing through the pines, but he could hear no other sounds.

When Old Snorter had finished her oats, she turned towards Tiger and touched him with her nose. After that she stood still and at last let her head drop and began to doze.

At last Tiger felt very tired. He was hungry for grass, but he became so sleepy that he dropped his head half-way to his knees and dozed like his mother. He felt that he had come to a very strange place. The man who had handled him was a strange creature, and so were the other men he had seen. This place where he was a prisoner was a complete mystery. But he was so hungry and tired that after he had dozed for a while he lay down at full length near his big mother and was soon sound asleep.

Old Snorter had been dozing for some time when she suddenly jerked her head up and listened. From the high land to the north of the stable beyond the hill she heard the wild howl of a wolf. Once again she heard the wolf howl, and after that there was no sound except the roaring of the wind through the tall pine trees.

Tiger slept peacefully on, but Old Snorter stood with her head up, listening. In her years of living in the wild she had learned the danger of the big grey wolves. She felt safe enough now, shut up with Tiger in the stable, but there was still something about the sound that kept her wide awake. She did not hear the wolf howl again and presently she dozed off, still standing.

It was a little before daylight when Tiger awakened. He raised his head and looked around him. He felt stronger after his rest but was still very hungry. He thrust out his long forelegs and rose up, his forepart first, and stood up on all four legs. He flipped his short tail a few times and yawned.

It was broad daylight when he and his mother

looked quickly towards the door. Someone was
fumbling with the outside latch. Then Tiger saw
the same strange two-legged creatures who had
led him there the day before.

Jim Summers and Buck Davis came in, locked
the door on the inside, and came over towards
Tiger. The colt snorted and backed away. Then
Jim went over to Old Snorter, patted her kindly,
and talked to her. He saw she had eaten her oats
and that Tiger also had finished his.

" You're learning, little feller," Jim said to him.

Jim picked up a halter and went up to Tiger.
The colt snorted and jumped back to a corner of
the stable. Jim and Buck both approached him
slowly. Tiger tried to leap out of the corner, but
Buck suddenly grabbed him around the neck with
his strong arms and held him. Jim began to put
the halter on Tiger's head, and although the colt
tried his best to break away, Buck was too strong
for him, and Jim succeeded in getting the halter
on. Both men were grinning, and Buck said, " Jim,
it looks as if he's going to be a bucker."

When two weeks had passed, Tiger was no
longer afraid of Jim when he came out to the
stable to see him, and after that he was taken out-

side and tied on a long rope. He soon learned not to run against the rope, because he did it a few times and was thrown down. So Tiger was tied out every day where he could eat all the grass he wanted.

Meanwhile, Jim took Old Snorter in hand and rode her almost every day on the range. He never wore spurs when riding her and he had no trouble with her. At night she was tied out on the grass far enough away from Tiger so that their ropes could not become entangled.

By the time fall came, Tiger was a beautiful black gelding with John Sheridan's brand on his shoulder. Jim had taught him to kneel and to get up at command. He also taught him to shake hands, when told to do so, by lifting a bent foreleg. Every evening Jim brought out some hard biscuits, and Tiger soon learned that he could earn one of the biscuits by obeying Jim's commands.

One evening John Sheridan watched Jim putting Tiger through his tricks. " Not many colts his age could learn like that," he said. " I've seen a few but not many. He's a mighty smart little horse."

Old Snorter was in a corral nearby, where Jim

had put her. Later, he would tie her out to graze. She seemed more restless than usual. She would gallop swiftly around the corral and then stop suddenly and stand still with her head up and her eyes shining. John Sheridan noticed the way she was behaving. " Jim," he said, " that old mare hasn't settled down much, even now, after all this time. I believe she'd still run away if she got loose and if Tiger would follow her."

The men stood looking at Old Snorter in the corral. " That old mare is plumb good," Buck said, " but I'd never trust her to stand alone. She's tame enough, but I notice she's generally looking away off towards the far places. I think she stays with us because Tiger is here. Now and then there's an old mare like that. She wants to be near her last colt even after he's getting big."

Soon winter came with its cold and snow. Both Old Snorter and Tiger were comfortable in the stable, and both were in fine condition when spring arrived. Tiger was almost full-grown now. He was a great favourite with all the men, but he was not interested in any of them except Jim. From the first, Jim had taken charge of his training, and Tiger felt that Jim was his master. When Jim came out of the house in the morning, Tiger would nicker for him, and every day Jim brought him a present—one or two hard biscuits or a lump of sugar.

By the last of May, Tiger had shed his winter coat and was a beautiful, shining black. He was still too young to ride much, but Jim got him used to the feel of the bridle and saddle, and one day he put his foot in the stirrup and carefully got up on Tiger's back. Tiger did not seem to mind but he did not know what Jim wanted him to do. Jim tapped him on the shoulder and said, " Go ahead, Tiger." But he still did not understand. Buck went back to the house, got some biscuits, and stood off a little way. When Jim said, " Go ahead, Tiger," Buck held out a biscuit. Tiger walked up to him and got it. They repeated this several times, and then when Jim tapped Tiger on the shoulder and told him to go ahead, he walked forward at once even though there was no biscuit for him. After that Jim rode Tiger round the ranch at a walk almost every day.

Frost came early the next fall and turned the buffalo grass on the range from a pale green to brown. This wild grass cured on the ground and made good feed through the winter. When it was covered with snow, a horse could paw down to it through the snow and get his food all winter. In those days the wild horses of the West were able to live very well through the longest and coldest winters by feeding on this wild buffalo grass.

One mild October night, all the horses on the ranch had been turned loose in a large corral except Tiger and Old Snorter. They were shut in a small corral by themselves. Jim did this because he felt that although Tiger was now a two-year-old, he was still too young to be turned loose in the big corral with the other horses. Some of them might kick him or even bite him.

This night, when Old Snorter saw that the light had at last gone out in the ranch house, she began to show signs of unusual restlessness. She walked rapidly round and round the small corral, now and then stopping and putting her nose close to the gate. Time and again she came up to Tiger, put her nose near him, and snorted gently. Soon Tiger also began to feel a sense of restlessness. He did not understand, but he knew that something was exciting his big mother. He followed her around in the corral at a fast walk, and now and then he snorted as she did.

Then Old Snorter began to trot around the corral, her head and tail high. A stiff wind was blowing away from the house towards the corral. Because of this and because the corral was about a hundred yards from the ranch house, none of the men were awakened by the sounds made by Tiger and the old mare.

The sky began to fill with small floating clouds and the night grew darker. The wind was blowing in a continual stiff breeze, making a steady roaring sound in the grove of tall pines beyond the corral.

By this time Old Snorter and Tiger were both prancing around. Tiger did not know the meaning of all this sudden action on the part of his old mother but the more he ran round with her, the more he was filled with excitement. He wanted action, the more the better.

Now Old Snorter made up her mind. Starting from the far side of the corral, she ran with great speed straight at the gate, striking the bars with her powerful chest. The gate crashed open. In an instant she was galloping away towards the west and Tiger, tingling with excitement, ran with her.

He had no difficulty in keeping up with her, for now his speed was equal to hers.

For several miles they raced across rolling country with clumps of trees and bushes here and there. Old Snorter led the way, now galloping down in a low place, then up on the other side, with Tiger close behind her. He did not know the meaning of all this, but he had a feeling he should follow on while Old Snorter led the way and he also felt a trace of the wild spirit that he had known before the men had caught him. After they had covered many miles, Old Snorter slowed down to a walk, and Tiger, tired by his long run, was glad to move more slowly too.

In due time they reached the head of Black Hawk Gorge. In this gorge, as in many others, tall trees grew up from the bottom. There were also small trees, many of them covered by thick, clinging vines. The frost had killed almost all the leaves on the trees, but withered leaves still clung on the dense vines and provided a rude shelter.

When Old Snorter, with Tiger close behind her, reached the head of Black Hawk Gorge, she stopped on a high spot and looked towards the northwest. She saw a great, dark cloud there and heard the distant rumble of thunder. Having lived for years in the wild, she knew what was coming and she also knew where to hunt for shelter.

She stood looking at the cloud for a few seconds, then started down the side of the gorge with Tiger following. It was so steep that they slid part of the way. Tiger came down right behind Old Snorter, his front legs braced out in front of him, sliding past the bushes in the loose earth. Tiger did not like this descent, because he felt he might lose his footing and roll helplessly down the steep bank. He snorted as he moved down behind his big mother.

When they reached the bottom, Old Snorter stopped to look around at Tiger and then started along the ravine. There were frequent rumbles of thunder and, as the clouds moved overhead, the night became very dark. The wise old mare had long been familiar with places like this ravine. She knew that there were often precipitous banks on the sides, under which a horse could stand and be partly protected from a fierce storm.

The mare had not gone far down the gorge when she suddenly stopped. By chance, she had come upon a place that offered some shelter. A huge tree, growing on the steep slope, had been broken by wind or lightning. It had fallen in such a way that the top was on the ground in the ravine and the broken trunk was wedged against a shelf of rock part way up the side. Great masses of vines had grown over the fallen tree all the way up to the rocky ledge.

Old Snorter pushed in under the vine-covered trunk of the tree, forcing her way still farther in when she felt Tiger's shoulder pushing her from the rear. She then let him stand next to the bank.

Ever since the moment when his big mother had crashed through the gate of the small corral, Tiger had been so full of the excitement of running wild and free that he had felt no fear or uneasiness over leaving Jim and the ranch home where he had been cared for so well. The instincts of a wild animal which he had had when he was a colt running on the range with Old Snorter had begun to come back to him. Tiger had forgotten all those wild feelings while he was living on the ranch because of the way Jim had worked with him, and if Old Snorter had not made her sudden break for freedom, Tiger would never have left Jim. If he had been even one year older, he probably would not have run any great distance with Old Snorter, for by that time his affection for Jim would have been stronger than his longing for freedom. As it was, though Tiger himself was not aware of this, he would never forget the kindness shown him by Jim in the only home he had ever known.

The thunder rumbled louder and louder. A flash of lightning glared in the gorge, followed by a deafening clap of thunder. Tiger and Old Snorter both jumped and then stood trembling. The mare was not greatly troubled, for she had lived through many such storms during her years in the wild. But to Tiger, who had spent more than half of his two years in the shelter of the ranch stables or corrals, this was a terrifying experience.

When Old Snorter found their shelter under the fallen tree, she had not noticed anything suspicious about the place. She would have been extremely wary if she had seen it. But because of the darkness and her eagerness to escape from the storm and the driving rain, she had not seen a large hole in the base of the bank under the tree trunk.

The cold October rain beat down in torrents.

The big trunk of the tree, the ledge of rock, and the dense tangle of vines broke some of the force of the storm, but now the rain was leaking through. Tiger was wet and cold, and the strangeness of his situation made him more and more uneasy. His mother was much less nervous, only making now and then a low snort of protest.

All unknown to Old Snorter and Tiger, the hole at the base of the bank beside which they stood had been used for several weeks past by a lone timber wolf. Old Snorter had caught no trace of wolf scent because of the rain.

The big wolf had been caught out in the storm, but now he had reached the ravine and was running for his den. The heavy rain also prevented him from smelling Old Snorter and Tiger.

It all happened in an instant. In the black darkness and the driving rain, the big wolf rushed for his den and found the entrance blocked by a large animal. Instinctively, the wolf slashed at Old Snorter and gashed her front leg. With a wild squeal of fear and rage she struck out with a powerful front hoof and, by chance, caught the wolf square on the head. He went down to stay, but Old Snorter, in desperate fear because of the strong wolf scent and the pain, pounded him again and again with her hoofs while she uttered piercing squeals of fright. Then she leaped out from the shelter and Tiger, terror-stricken by the scent and by his mother's actions, leaped out behind her. She ran a short distance in the blinding rain and then plunged into some tall clumps of brush and stopped. Tiger ran against her and stood trembling. Old Snorter turned and faced towards the spot where she had met the big wolf.

Tiger did not know what had happened, but he was frightened and miserable. He stood with his side pressing against Old Snorter's. He had never before known such terror except on the day when he had been captured by men and had felt their hands on him, and he had long ago forgotten about that. As he stood there in the tall brush with Old Snorter, the cold rain drenching him, Tiger's mind was like that of a wild thing. He thought only of self-preservation.

Now and then he shook his head and blew through his nostrils as the rain ran down over his face. Old Snorter also felt the rain on her face, but she kept her head up, staring out in the black darkness to see or smell the dangerous enemy that had rushed in to attack her. Tiger waited, miserable and anxious in the roar of the storm.

At last both the rain and lightning ceased and only distant mutterings of thunder could be heard. Then there was complete silence except for the rippling of the water as it flowed along the bottom of the gorge, which before the storm had been a dry, sandy stream bed. Already the sky was clear and thousands of stars were twinkling.

Old Snorter was wise to the ways of the wild. She knew that wolves usually travelled in packs and that there might be many more of them in the gorge. She wanted to be on open land. With a snort, she pushed out of the brush and stood still for a minute, looking, smelling the air, and listening. She could see nothing but the dark clumps of brush and the leafless trees standing silent in the gorge. With another snort, she started towards the head of the ravine, looking for a slope up which she and Tiger could scramble and get out to open ground. She soon came to a place where she knew they could go up. She lunged up the steep slope with Tiger scrambling and plunging after her.

When she gained the open land above, Old

Snorter whirled to see whether Tiger was making the difficult climb. She saw his head and shoulders near the top and then he made the final plunge that brought him to the level ground above the gorge. Old Snorter at once started off at a fast trot. She rounded the point where the gorge dipped down in the hills, and broke into a gallop. Tiger galloped behind her, glad of the exercise after having been chilled by the cold rain.

Now that Old Snorter at last found herself free in the wild, she was anxious to get as far as possible from the spot where she and Tiger had been prisoners. She knew she was headed towards new country and she turned and travelled for many miles towards the west.

CHAPTER FIVE

A FIGHT WITH WOLVES

OLD SNORTER was elated to be free at last and even happier to have her son running beside her. She had seen Tiger every evening while they had been at the ranch, and her love for him had grown stronger than ever. Now, as they galloped together, all she wanted was this new freedom to run the range with Tiger.

Her first thought was to get as far away from the men at the ranch as possible, so she led Tiger on for many miles before she let him stop. The young horse finally began to lag behind, and Old Snorter decided that it was time to stop and eat the excellent buffalo grass that grew everywhere around them. Tiger was even hungrier than his mother, and he ate the grass greedily. It seemed especially delicious to him after his long gallop.

Old Snorter and Tiger travelled on for a number of days. The nourishing buffalo grass kept Tiger in fine condition. Frequently he would have liked to stop and graze for a longer time, but the mare would grow impatient and urge him on.

Late one evening, after they had been grazing for several hours, Old Snorter threw up her head. She was ready to move again. She came walking briskly up to Tiger, stopped and looked at him, and then turned to gaze off into the distance. Blowing once through her nostrils, she put her nose against Tiger's and started at a rapid walk towards the south. It was just as if she were saying, " Come on, son, we must be going."

After travelling for a mile, they reached the foot of a high hill. There was a deep cut in the hill that offered good shelter from the chill wind which was steadily blowing. Old Snorter walked into the cut and stopped. Tiger followed and stood beside her. The colt felt comfortable and was glad to have the chance to rest. He stood quietly looking out on the plain, but there was nothing to see except the silent land itself. As he became sleepy, his head dropped lower and lower. Old Snorter could not doze with her colt, however, for she felt uneasy remaining in one spot. As long as they were moving, she felt that they could keep their freedom, and she was eager to leave the ranch as far behind as possible. So while Tiger slept, the old mare kept watch, alert for any strange sights or sounds. When the stars faded from the sky and daylight came, she led Tiger through the cut in the hill and on towards the southwest.

Old Snorter and Tiger travelled on for weeks, living on the plentiful buffalo grass. The weather was still exceptionally mild, but the hard winter would surely strike soon.

One night in December, Old Snorter and Tiger took shelter in a ravine. They had been able to drink at a small stream which ran along the bottom of the ravine and emptied into a river not far below. Tiger and Old Snorter could hear the steady roar of the wind as it blew through the tops of the giant trees in the bottom of the ravine. By midnight the sky was completely overcast with heavy dark clouds, and the north wind was cold. Tiger snorted and stepped about to keep warm. The chill air was laden with moisture which made the cold even harder to bear.

About two o'clock in the morning a fine misty rain began falling. There had been no snow so far this winter, but the cold fine mist was almost as uncomfortable. The cold increased and finally ice began to form on the bare branches of the trees. If it had not been for the heat in their bodies, ice would even have formed on the coats of the two horses.

There seemed to be no life in the cold and lonely ravine except for the two black horses who were seeking shelter there. Suddenly an owl, hidden by the darkness, came flying through the chilling mist and lighted in a big tree. There was a hole in the trunk, and the owl edged along a limb until it reached this shelter. It perched on the rim of the hole, peered out into the darkness, and cried, "Whoo! Whoo!" Then it settled back, its body protected by the hollow.

Tiger started at the loud, lonely call of the owl, but Old Snorter only pricked up her ears. She had long ago become accustomed to such noises in the stillness of the night, and they did not bother her now. The wind kept roaring constantly through the tall trees, and before dawn loud cracking sounds could be heard. Ice had formed on all the branches of the trees, and as the wind bent the limbs, the ice splintered and split apart.

A low bank provided some shelter from the cold north wind and the chilling mist for Tiger and Old Snorter, but the young horse still felt cold, wet, and miserable. He was tired, too, and finally he dozed off into a fitful sleep. Vague memories of Jim and the ranch stable came back to him, and he dreamed of the comfort and security he had known there. He could not remember those days in the way that a person can remember his childhood, but he was filled with an uneasy feeling that he had known a place where there was food and warmth and peace, a place where he had not been afraid of the world around him.

The night passed slowly, but Old Snorter did not doze. She kept her head up and her eyes open, alert for any possible danger. As morning came, the wind died away and finally ceased, and when it was daylight there were only a few clouds in the sky. The sunlight filtered down into the gorge, and Tiger saw a wonderland around him. Everything was frozen and still, and each tree and bush was coated with a film of ice that gleamed and sparkled in the light of the morning. But Tiger and his mother were unaware of the beauty, feeling only the lifeless and forbidding cold.

Tiger stared all around him and noticed the strange way the trees and bushes glittered in the morning sun. Old Snorter, however, turned quickly away from this unusual spectacle and touched Tiger on the neck with her nose. She tossed her head and told him with her character-istic snort that it was time to start walking up the ravine. They followed the edge of the small stream, which was still flowing, although ice had formed at its edges. The ground on both sides of the stream was covered with patches of thin ice. It was not strong enough to hold the weight of Old Snorter and Tiger, and their hoofs broke through at every step.

The drooping limbs of the ice-covered trees, brushed Old Snorter's back as she walked along and showers of tiny ice crystals went cascading to the ground. Finally they reached a place where the mare decided they could plunge up the slope and reach the top of the ravine. She leaped for-ward, with Tiger close behind, and broke through the bushes which grew thickly all the way to the top. Paying no attention to the showers of ice they left behind them, the two horses were soon on the open land, which the past night had transformed into an astonishing sight. The plain had become a sea of shining glass, and they paused in surprise under the low-hanging boughs of a tree while Old Snorter decided what to do.

They were hungry after the long hard night, but now the buffalo grass was hidden under ice. Old Snorter, however, remembered from previous winters what to do. Soon she walked out to a patch of ice, sniffed at it, and struck it with her big hoof several times. The ice splintered and she found the grass underneath, just as she had hoped, and began to eat ravenously. Tiger came over to her and began to eat the grass she had uncovered. When she went a little distance away and cleared another patch of grass, he watched and understood. Then he began to break the thin ice with his own hoofs and soon was grazing on the delicious grass unaided.

Wild range horses would never have been able to live through Western winters if they had not known that there was grass to eat under the ice and snow. Thousands of cattle died each winter just because they could not find food after the snow came. Ice storms made eating more difficult, but a horse's hoof could almost always break through the crust.

It was a clear morning, full of winter sunshine, but so cold that the ice did not melt. By noontime Old Snorter and Tiger had stopped pawing for the grass and were content to stand and rest on the glistening ground. Gradually the day began to grow warmer, and by late afternoon the thin ice had started to melt. Tiger was glad to feel the change, for he had been cold all night and all morning, too. As he and his mother stood on the icy plain, they looked like two jet-black dots on an endless field of frozen white.

Old Snorter felt restless when the weather grew warmer, and she began to walk. There was still a crust of ice on the ground, and the crunching noises she and Tiger made were the only sounds to be heard in the quietness of the winter afternoon. They rounded the head of the gorge, and Old Snorter stopped to gaze towards the west. Tiger looked also, but he could see nothing. All he knew was that he was safe with his mother, and he reached out to touch Old Snorter's shoulder with his nose. As she continued walking towards the west, Tiger followed her closely. He could see buffalo grass all around him now, for large patches of ice had melted away.

After walking several miles, they came to a rise in the ground and saw a long narrow valley stretched out below them. A clump of trees in the centre of the valley sheltered an abandoned ranch-house, and they could see a small corral and a stable nearby. But what held Old Snorter's attention most of all was a sizeable stack of hay that had been left there. The ranchman had probably put up hay for saddle stock kept at the ranch during the winter, and then for some reason he had moved away and left it behind.

Old Snorter paused for only a moment and then led the way down the slope and into the deserted ranch yard. She walked once round the house, went to the corral, and sniffed the ground. She knew immediately that there were no men around and that this ranch would be a safe shelter.

Tiger watched curiously while his mother investigated the place, but when she walked up to the haystack, thrust her nose well in, and drew forth a large mouthful of good hay, he hurried to her side. He had not realised until then what a feast was in store for him. The hay had been cut from a valley of tall, rich meadow grass, and even though the stack was a year old, there was nourishing hay under the outer covering.

When they had eaten their fill, Old Snorter headed towards a river about half a mile away. The bank on their side sloped gently, and they were able to reach the water's edge without any difficulty. They both drank for a long time without stopping, until finally Old Snorter raised her head and gazed across the river. Tiger followed her glance for a moment but decided he was more interested in the water, and drank again. A colt needs more food and more water than a fully grown horse, so Tiger stayed at the river's edge long after Old Snorter was ready to leave. Finally he was satisfied and they both started back towards the ranch and the haystack.

Old Snorter and Tiger were content to remain at this place. The mare knew instinctively that colder weather would be coming soon and that the haystack and the stable would help them survive the winter. That evening a sudden blast of cold wind came down from the north and filled Old Snorter with concern. When she looked in the direction of the wind, she saw a vast, dark cloud looming in the distance.

Tiger trembled violently in the chilling blast, and turned to watch the coming storm. Both horses quickly left the haystack and walked to the stable. The door was broken and hung open, so Old Snorter thrust her head inside and looked around. The stable was deserted, as she had thought it would be, and she walked inside, with Tiger following close behind. The door was the only opening, and it was on the south side, away from the winter winds.

The wind grew colder and fiercer, and then the first flurry of snow appeared. It came down gently at first, but the noise of the wind became louder and louder every moment. It was calm inside the stable, however, and Tiger and Old Snorter felt secure from the blasts of the cold wind. They stood a little back from the door, watching the fine, spitting snow driven along by the fierce wind.

Then in one startling instant the picture changed. The snow came down like a blanket and the day became almost as dark as night. Old Snorter tossed her head anxiously, snorting at the darkness outside. Tiger was terrified and backed quickly to the rear of the stable in his desire to run away from the mystifying sight in front of him. However, he knew that he was sheltered, and the presence of his mother reassured him. He realised that it would be best to remain quietly with her.

Harder and fiercer, the blizzard drove against the stable. What had been a mild day had turned suddenly into one of the wildest and most deadly storms that had ever swept the range. No living thing could have survived this storm without shelter. The temperature had now dropped far below zero and the cold penetrated through the walls of the stable. Tiger and Old Snorter both shivered violently and kept stepping about, trying to keep their blood circulating as the long hours passed.

The wind did not die down as the time went by, and the dangerous blizzard raged on as if it would never cease. All that night Old Snorter and Tiger moved about restlessly in the stable, too cold to sleep. Swirls of snow blew inside the door- way, but since the storm was coming from the north, the interior of the stable was protected from much of the snow and wind.

Morning finally came, bringing no change. The

inky blackness became a little lighter, but the snow was still so thick that a man out in the storm could not have seen more that a few feet in front of him. The blizzard roared on for the whole day, and Tiger and Old Snorter had to walk around continually to keep from freezing in the stabbing cold.

The day passed, night came again, and even on the second day the blizzard was still raging. During the second night the storm reached its height. The wind howled around the stable as if it were determined to destroy the two horses that so far had been shielded from the full fury of its blasts. But late in the night Old Snorter noticed a change. The wind grew quieter, and soon she and Tiger no longer heard its terrible roar. Then the sky began to clear and a gentler wind moaned and sighed around the corners of the stable. The terrifying sounds had faded, but it was still bitterly cold.

The morning revealed a shining, white, frozen world that was too dazzling to look at long. Old Snorter walked through the snow that had blown in the doorway and stepped outside into the deep drifts. Walking was very difficult, but Tiger crowded close behind her. Both horses were too hungry and thirsty to be timid about leaving their shelter. They immediately went to the haystack, which was now a huge mound of white snow. On the north side the drifts were higher than their heads, and even on the south side the snow was above Old Snorter's knees. Nevertheless, she plunged through on that side, thrust her nose into the stack, and drew out a large mouthful of the fine, bright hay. Tiger instantly followed her example, and began to eat so hastily that he devoured both the hay and the snow that covered it.

Even though the snow provided some water, the two horses could not eat much without finding a pool or stream to quench their thirst. Old Snorter backed away from the hay and looked towards the river. It had not seemed far away before, but now she knew it would be hard to reach. She snorted at Tiger and then started out, as if to say, " Come on, son. We've got to find some water."

The sun was bright in the clear sky, but the wind was bitterly cold. The two horses shivered as they made their way across the range. They found that in some places the wind had swept the level ground almost bare of snow, but in other spots enormous drifts had piled up. Old Snorter was able to go around most of these, but now and then she and Tiger had to flounder through one. More than once the snow came up to their necks, but somehow they managed to get through.

With great relief they finally came to the gentle slope that marked the bank of the river, but they stopped short at the sight of the solidly frozen stream. There were great patches of snow on part of the ice, but there were also large areas of bare ice which glistened in the sun.

Old Snorter went down to the edge of the ice and started to walk out on it very carefully. Tiger followed her, but he did not realise that the frozen surface was so slippery and he fell to his knees. Old Snorter halted and waited till she saw him get up. She blew gently through her nose then, as if she were trying to say, " Be careful, son. Watch your step here."

Not far from the bank the limb of a dead tree struck up through the ice. The mare instinctively knew that this would be the most likely spot for her to reach the water. She walked over to the limb and looked at the ice around it. Just as she had hoped, the ice was thinner here, and she could even see the water moving below it. Old Snorter stood close to the limb and brought her heavy front hoof down on the ice as hard as she could. Her hoof broke the ice and went into the water, making a hole large enough for drinking. She immediately began to drink, and Tiger cautiously came up beside her. He put his nose down and they drank together. They spent a long time at the river, for they had been without water during all the storm. They would drink for a time, and then pause for a few moments to look across the river. When they were satisfied at last, they cautiously turned back to the ranch.

Tiger was still not used to the snow and twice he fell to his knees. Each time Old Snorter stopped and watched him while he struggled to his feet. When they reached the open land, it was easier to move, and Old Snorter started back at a gallop, trying to keep warm. Tiger ran eagerly, for he had been confined too long without exercise.

They spent the rest of the day at the haystack, and when evening came they went back into the stable. It had been cold all day long, but now the cold grew even more intense, and they were grateful for the shelter. For three days and three nights after the storm Old Snorter and Tiger stayed near the haystack, making daily trips to the river for water. Each time the mare was able to break the ice around the limb and clear a space for drinking.

In the years when Old Snorter had run wild, she had survived other hard winters. She had always been able to find food, but sometimes it had been hard work to paw through the deep snow to uncover the buffalo grass. Now that she had found this stack of good hay, she decided to remain near it during the bitter weather. The days continued to be cold, and now and then a driving snow would hide the range from view. Old Snorter and Tiger protected themselves, however, by sleeping in the stable every night, and December and January slowly passed by.

One night in early February the two horses were in the stable as usual. It was bitterly cold, and a freezing wind swept down from the north over the bleak countryside. Tiger, who had become accustomed to his lonely surroundings, was lying down and dozing. He could never lie down for long at a time, because it was too cold, but he had been on his feet for several hours and now he was resting. His head was up but his nose almost touched the ground. Old Snorter had taken her usual position facing the open doorway. Even when she dozed she remained on her feet, so that she would be ready for any possible danger.

Around midnight Old Snorter suddenly awoke with a start. Her head jerked up and her eyes opened wide. She could see small swirls of snow that the wind was driving across the land, but they were not the cause of her fear. She had heard frightening sounds, and now she listened for them to come again. At that moment the weird howls of a wolf pack echoed through the night, and she gave a loud snort which awakened Tiger. He was puzzled at first, but then he too heard the wild howls.

Tiger was frightened and leaped to his feet. He did not know what the sounds meant, for he had never met a grey wolf, but he instinctively felt that danger was near. Old Snorter, however, had been through many experiences with wolves. There were scars on both her hind legs where wolves had tried without success to snap her hamstrings. She knew exactly what the danger was when she realised that wolves were hunting close to the stable, but she had fought them before and she would fight them again.

The wolves were coming down the river with the wind behind them, and each howl was sharp and distinct in the clear night. Old Snorter whirled and turned in the direction of the noise. Tiger, even more alarmed by his mother's actions, faced in the same direction, and together they waited to see if they would be discovered. Suddenly the howling ceased, and the silence frightened the horses even more than the strident wolf chorus. It meant that the wolves had come across the tracks of Old Snorter and Tiger at their drinking place on the river.

There were four huge grey wolves in the pack, and they all stopped when they found the horses' trail. They looked in the direction of the stable and with one accord started to run along the trail. They moved quickly in great leaps, but not a sound could be heard except for the pad of their feet on the snow. When they drew near the ranch house and stable, they stopped and sniffed the air, for buildings usually meant that men were nearby. Their keen sense of smell told them instantly that no men were here. At the same time they caught the strong scent of Old Snorter and Tiger and knew that the horses were hiding in the stable. The wolves grew more and more excited, for they did not find horseflesh to feast upon very often.

The savage beasts cautiously crept into the yard. They were panting after their run and their long red tongues hung out. Seeing a big horse and a smaller one guarding the doorway of the stable, they decided to circle it, hoping to find another entrance. The open doorway was the only way to reach the horses, however, and the two boldest wolves made a sudden rush at the opening. Their attack was so swift that one of them might have got in, but Old Snorter caught the first one on the head with her front hoof and crushed its skull.

Tiger, terror-stricken though he was, struck hard at the other wolf, and hit it on the side of the head. The wolf shrank back and joined the others, but they had not given up yet. The three wolves held back from the doorway for a moment with their heads low, their tongues lolling out, and a deadly gleam in their eyes. Old Snorter was angry now, and she squealed again and again as she continued to stamp on the wolf lying at her feet. Tiger began to catch his mother's spirit and, with eyes blazing, he snorted his defiance. The three wolves changed their strategy and disappeared around one side of the stable. Tiger and Old Snorter did not move, but they poked their heads farther out of the doorway so that they would be sure to see everything that happened. There was a moment of tense silence in which the two horses could see nothing but the snow in the starlight and could hear only the moaning and sighing of the wind.

In a flash all three wolves leaped around the corner and charged the doorway together. The sounds of horses squealing and wolves snarling filled the bleak winter night. The flailing hoofs of both Tiger and Old Snorter would have discouraged most wolves, but these were hungry and desperate, and the horses had to fight with every bit of strength they possessed.

Two wolves were struck down, and now the third shrank aside with a broken shoulder and tried to limp away. Tiger and Old Snorter pounded the two wolves in the doorway until their fury was spent, and then Old Snorter leaped out into the snow to catch up with the remaining wolf. The beast turned and snarled. Old Snorter squealed in rage as she struck the wolf with a front hoof. It fell immediately but the mare was not satisfied until she had pounded it into the snow for several minutes. When she stopped, she stood still and cocked her ears to listen for any other warning sounds. There might be other wolves prowling in the night, and she listened intently for a long time. Tiger timidly left the stable and listened too.

The night seemed peaceful, and both walked back to the doorway. One of the wolves lay across their path and Tiger was afraid to step over it. He knew it was harmless now, but he had not recovered from the fear he had felt during the fight. Old Snorter leaped in and kicked hard with both hind hoofs, lifting the dead wolf from the ground and knocking it ten feet out on the snow. Tiger then stepped quickly through the doorway. Though the danger had passed, neither of the horses could sleep. They remained in the doorway, looking out and listening.

After standing guard all night, Tiger was extremely tired. But when daylight came he was too hungry to sleep, and he went to the haystack with his mother. At noon Old Snorter led the way to the river, over the lifeless snowy wastes. Tiger knew the procedure by now, and he confidently followed his mother to the place where the tree limb protruded from the ice. He waited while she broke the surface and then drank eagerly. The return trip to the haystack was uneventful, and they ate there until late afternoon. When it began to grow dark, they went into the stable and finally were able to rest. They were beginning to forget the terrible struggle of the night before.

They stayed at the ranch all the rest of the winter and neither heard nor saw any more wolves. By the middle of March the snow began to melt and bare patches of ground could be seen. Now the horses were no longer dependent on the haystack for food, and they wandered over the nearby highland, where they were able to graze on buffalo grass. Towards evening Old Snorter always led the way back to the stable.

By mid-April all the snow had disappeared except in a few places where the deepest drifts had been. A few weeks later Old Snorter and her son left the stable for good. She and Tiger travelled for miles the first day, grazing where they found good clumps of grass. When night came they stopped beside a clear flowing stream and drank the cool water. A large willow tree grew on the bank, and they spent the night under its drooping branches.

Signs of life began to appear on the range now. Big long-eared jack rabbits scurried across their path, and occasionally they saw a coyote slink away in the distance. The whistle of redbirds came from the trees along the streams and in the deep wooded ravines, and meadow larks sent forth their clear notes in the grassland of the valleys.

Old Snorter and Tiger were not travelling steadily in any one direction now, but they kept moving every day. Tiger felt contented enough, but it was a lonely existence. He had experienced something in his months with Jim Summers that he would never quite forget. During all the hardships and dangers of the winter he had not thought of the peaceful life with Jim. But on these spring nights, when there was no longer anything to fear, sometimes a dim memory of the ranch and Jim would come to him, and he would have a feeling that he wanted to be back at that place where Jim was. Then he would raise his head high and look all around him towards the far dark horizon.

Jim Summers and Buck Davis had hunted far and wide for Tiger after he and Old Snorter had broken out of the corral, but to their great disappointment they found no trace of him. It was the same on other distant ranches where Jim rode to inquire. Not a man had seen either Old Snorter or her beautiful black colt.

Meanwhile Old Snorter and Tiger roamed free. The mare was satisfied, for she was now living the kind of life she liked best. But Tiger was not wholly content. While he was still quite young something had come into his life that had left its mark on him. He wanted to be with his mother more than any other horse, yet he was not satisfied in the wild as the defiant, independent old mare was. It had been natural for him to run away with Old Snorter the night when she broke down the corral gate, and everything he had done since then had been determined by the strong instinct of self-preservation. But now it was also natural for him to be restless and lonely at times.

He wandered on with Old Snorter, grazing fairly near her during the day and standing close beside her at night wherever she decided it was safe to stop. There was still some danger of attack by the big grey wolves, and Old Snorter usually spent the night on a wide, open plain where she could see everything all around her.

One morning, after they had grazed on a highland, Old Snorter led Tiger down into a small, narrow valley where the grass was exceedingly thick and good. She and Tiger began grazing near a clump of timber by the small creek that flowed through the valley.

It happened that two cowboys were hiding in the woods near the stream at that very moment. Not long before, as they rode up out of the valley, they had seen Old Snorter and Tiger grazing on the highland nearby. The men quickly wheeled their horses and rode back down into the valley. They concealed themselves and their horses in the woods, believing that the two black horses they had seen might come down later to drink at the stream.

Old Snorter and Tiger did not see them, and since the breeze was blowing towards the men, the mare and her colt got no scent of them. When after a time, Old Snorter and Tiger did come down over the hill for a drink at the little creek, they had no warning of the presence of the men and horses hidden in the trees. Both cowboys held their rifles ready, hoping to crease the two fine black horses, if possible. This meant grazing the top of a horse's neck with a bullet—knocking him down and dazing him for a moment but not otherwise injuring him. While the horse was down, the men would run up, tie him with a rope, and capture him. It took a fine marksman to do this, and both these men were excellent shots with a rifle.

They waited expectantly while Old Snorter and Tiger came down the hill and began to graze. Presently the two beautiful black horses came towards the creek to drink. They came on, walking steadily with no suspicion of danger, until they reached the edge of the creek. They put their heads down and drank from the clear running water.

The men wanted to capture both horses but they especially wanted Tiger. They saw that he was young and graceful. Old Snorter was fine and powerful too, but Tiger was the more beautiful horse of the two.

Old Snorter and Tiger finished drinking and lifted their heads briefly to look around them. Tiger stood on the far side of the mare so that the riflemen had no chance at him. They waited, hoping that both the black horses would move out a little way and become separated while grazing.

Presently Old Snorter and Tiger did walk out a little distance on the level ground and begin to graze. But Tiger, by chance, stayed on the far side of his mother. The men still waited, ready to shoot the instant both horses were in the right position. However, Tiger gave them no chance at him. He began to graze away from Old Snorter down the valley with his back directly towards the men.

Old Snorter raised her head for an instant and turned her side towards the men, exposing herself in just the way they wanted. They were afraid she might turn again and follow Tiger so that they would have no further chance to get either horse. A rifle cracked and Old Snorter fell to the ground. Tiger jerked up his head to see the two men running towards his mother. He leaped away and ran like a streak down the valley.

When he had run a good distance and felt safe, he stopped, whirled about, and looked back. The two men were standing near Old Snorter, who was up on her feet again. Each man had a rope around her neck and both were holding her while she jumped and plunged about. But knowing men and their ropes as she did, Old Snorter soon gave up. Tiger presently saw the two men leading her, one on either side, towards the grove of trees. In a little while he saw the men mounted on their own horses, leading Old Snorter away up the valley. Tiger sent forth a loud, piercing nicker to his mother. She tried to turn about but the men prevented her from doing so. Then she called back to Tiger with a shrill nicker. The men hoped he would follow so that they might capture him later, but Tiger was too frightened. The sound of the rifle and the actions of the men as they rushed up and captured Old Snorter had filled him with such terror that all he wanted was to get as far from them as possible.

CHAPTER SIX

CAUGHT BY HORSE THIEVES

SPRING HAD come again. Alone, Tiger had lived through another winter in the wild.

Far from the Sheridan ranch, in a remote and lonely region, a band of horse thieves had made their camp, planning to raid all the ranches in that part of the country. They had already stolen more than a dozen horses, and they planned to get as many more before they started their night drive to a distant market.

At the moment the stolen range horses were quietly grazing under the watchful eyes of Bill and Texas Pete, two of the rustlers. The others, a dozen in number, were rolled up in their blankets under the shadows of some trees a little distance away from the stolen horses.

On one side of the level grassland was a spring from which the water ran down into a small, clear pool. From time to time two or three of the horses would stop grazing to walk over to the pool for a drink of the clear, cold water. On both sides of the spring, about forty feet away, there grew dense clumps of cedar trees and some tall bushes.

The night was clear, with the moon and stars shining. It was about two o'clock in the morning and all the men except the two guards were sound asleep. Bill and Texas Pete were standing near the cedar trees, holding their saddled horses and talking to each other in low tones. Suddenly Pete exclaimed softly, " Look over there! " Bill looked where he was pointing, across on the opposite side of the level grassland where the horses were grazing. In the bright moonlight both men could see a big black horse walking slowly towards the others. As he drew nearer, they could see his long legs and his fine strong build, and they were sure that he must have tremendous speed. Not even a dozen men on smaller horses would be able to catch him if he decided to run away.

The horse was Black Tiger. By chance he had come within sight of the herd of horses, and after all the lonely months that had passed since his mother had been captured he wanted the companionship of his own kind.

Bill and Pete whispered quickly together, making a careful plan. If he were not frightened away, sometime during the night this great black horse would probably come up to the spring to drink. They would hide in the cedar trees near the spring and wait for him.

A light breeze was blowing from Tiger towards the hidden riders. They noted this and knew it was excellent for their purpose. They tied their horses to a tree deep in the grove and took the coils of both lariat ropes from the saddles. With the ropes on their arms, they stole through the woods towards the spring. Now and then they stopped to peep out of the shadows to see if the black horse was coming closer. They saw that he had come near the other horses and had stopped, standing with his head up and looking around as if he suspected some kind of danger.

The two men moved like slinking coyotes in the shadows of the trees, keeping behind bushes and clumps of trees until they reached the spring. On the ground in front of the pool they carefully placed two loops of rope, then took up their hiding place in the deep shadows of a thicket, near a tree only a little distance away. Each man held the end of his rope. If Tiger should step inside either one of the loops that lay on the ground, the rope would be jerked quickly and would catch him either by the front legs or the hind ones. The hidden men noted with satisfaction that the wind was still in their favour. They could see the stolen horses grazing in the moonlit valley, and presently they saw Tiger come up close to the others. They paid little attention to him but went on eating the grass, and he began to graze near them.

All was quiet about the place except for the sounds the horses made as they stepped along, biting off the green grass and now and then blowing softly through their nostrils. The gentle breeze blew steadily, whispering through the leafy thickets and the clumps of trees that stood like dark shadows in the lonely valley.

Tiger had felt thirsty when he first joined the other horses but, not knowing where the water was, he kept on grazing. After a while he happened to be near a grey horse, a little apart from the others. The grey horse lifted his head and chewed on a large mouthful of grass while he looked in the direction of the spring. Then he started walking steadily towards the spring and Tiger followed close behind him. All the other horses kept on grazing.

The grey horse walked on towards the spring, ignoring the surroundings because he had been there before. He saw the two loops of rope lying on the ground, but he paid no attention to them for they seemed as harmless as the quiet place itself.

When the grey horse came to the spring, he put his head down and began drinking. He stood with both front feet in one loop and with one of his hind feet in the other. He drank his fill and stood still for a few seconds as a horse will often do after he has finished drinking. Then he turned about and started slowly walking away. Now Tiger walked up to the spring and began drinking. He was quite thirsty and found the cool, clear water very refreshing. The wind, blowing away from him, did not give him the slightest warning of danger.

Suddenly something at his feet became alive. Tiger tried to leap back and whirl, but the evil gripping thing jerked hard on both his front legs and he fell to his knees. He tried to leap up, but the rope tightened and pulled hard on his legs, half-way between his hoofs and his knees, holding his two front legs together.

Bill quickly tied the end of his rope to a nearby tree. Texas Pete had jerked the other rope, hoping to catch Tiger by the hind legs with it, but he had not succeeded. Now he ran up quickly, and while Tiger struggled and floundered, trying to get his front feet apart, Pete tied his rope around Tiger's neck. Then he fastened the other end to the tree. Bill took the slip noose off Tiger's front legs and tied that end of his rope firmly around the horse's neck. Now Tiger was restrained by two stout ropes that would hold him but would not choke him. There was no possible escape. Tiger lunged back hard a few times against the two ropes and then, knowing it was useless, he stopped and stood still.

Bill and Pete were delighted with their prize. There was no doubt that Tiger was a more valuable horse than any other in the string they had stolen. Presently the two men saw that some of the horses had begun to wander too far away. They left Tiger where he was and hurried back to their own horses, which were still tied in the cedar grove. They untied them, mounted, and rode down in front of the straying horses, driving them back to the rest of the herd.

Just as Bill and Pete started to turn back towards the spring, a number of horses appeared on the hilltop and came down into the valley. Behind this new herd were two riders whom Bill and Pete recognised. They had left the day before, intending to ride to a ranch about twenty miles away and, if possible, steal a number of horses there. Bill and Pete rode out in the moonlight and greeted the newcomers in low tones. They reported that their raid had been successful, for they had brought back eight horses stolen from two different ranches. They rode their horses out on the grass, dismounted, and hobbled them, leaving the saddles on.

After Tiger saw that he could not break the two ropes that held him, he turned around and looked towards the other horses, all peacefully grazing in the moonlight some distance away. While he stood watching, three of them, a black-and-white spotted horse and two bays, came walking towards the spring to drink. The black-and-white spotted one, called a pinto, was in the lead and he stopped when quite near Tiger and looked at him. The two bay horses walked past the pinto and went on to the spring. Tiger snorted and was ill at ease, because the ropes made him a prisoner.

The pinto horse approached Tiger and suddenly laid back his ears. For an instant his teeth shone as he lunged forward and tried to bite Tiger. In a flash Tiger whirled and slammed both his hind hoofs against the pinto's ribs. The horse grunted and staggered back. Tiger snorted angrily and stood watching him. Meanwhile, the two bays walked to the spring, took a long drink, and went back into the valley. The pinto snorted once at the fighting black horse, but did not try to go past him to the spring. He went back to the other horses without drinking.

For a while all was still around Tiger except for the low wind that stirred through the thickets and the trees. All at once a creature that looked almost like the moonlight on the grass moved out from behind a clump of bushes and approached the spring. It was a brownish-grey coyote. Tiger snorted more in contempt than in fear. The coyote stopped, looked at the great black horse standing near, then gave up the notion of drinking, slunk out of sight beyond the bushes, and loped away.

Tiger began to step restlessly about. He felt a

great anxiety at being tied here. As yet the men had not hurt him much, but he had a strong fear of them. They had not been kind and friendly to him as Jim and the men on the Sheridan Ranch had always been.

In his uneasiness and fear, dim memories of Jim and the men he had grown up with came back to Tiger again. His head dropped a little and something stirred in his brain, recalling to him his life in happier circumstances. His present situation, with all that had happened before, was a complete mystery to him.

While Tiger stood, half dreaming, half awake, the stars began to pale. The moon was far down towards the western horizon. Morning was coming. The big black horse was facing towards the place where the horse rustlers had spent the night. Now that grey dawn had come, Tiger could see the men moving about and could hear them talking.

After a while an odour came to Tiger's nose. It was the smell of frying meat. He had often smelled the same odour at the Sheridan Ranch when he was with Jim, but this was the first time this smell had come to him in almost two years. He pricked up his ears and stood watching, for somehow the scent of frying meat was associated in his mind with Jim.

After some time, two other men rode down to the end of the valley to stand watch over the herd of horses, and Pete and Bill came back to the place where the men had prepared breakfast. The returning guards pointed out Black Tiger to the others at once. He was standing close to the tree now, and a bush partly concealed him. Bill and Texas Pete directed their talk mostly to the leader of the horse rustlers, a tall slim man with a black beard and beady, black eyes.

The tall leader stood up, and he and all the other men started walking up the low incline towards the spring. When they got near, Tiger leaped about and snorted, because he was afraid of them. All the rustlers exclaimed over the fine horse that Bill and Pete had caught. After some talk the leader said, " He's too wild to try to drive with the other horses. If he got loose and ran away, our whole outfit could not catch him. One of you will have to ride him."

These horse rustlers, like most of their kind, were skilled riders. They had to be, for often their lives depended on the speed of their horses and their skill in riding. They all saw, however, that if this great black horse, who was standing and glaring at them, proved to be a hard bucker, the best of them would find it difficult to stay on his back.

The two ropes tying Tiger to the tree were unfastened and two men held the end of each one as they started to lead him down to a wide, level piece of ground. In this way two men on each side of Tiger could hold him while some of the others tried to ride him. Both of these ropes which the men held were long.

As soon as the men untied the ropes from the tree and started to lead Tiger down to the level ground, he plunged and struggled to get away from them. But the four rustlers dug the high heels of their boots in the ground, quickly put the ropes half-way around their hips, and used their combined strength to hold him. It was not easy even for four of them to restrain the powerful black horse as he tried to rush first towards one side and then towards the other in his frantic efforts to escape.

When Tiger saw that he could not break away from the men, he stood still, breathing a little rapidly, his head held high, his ears moving restlessly forwards and backwards. Any intelligent horse acts this way when he is caught and is trying to figure out what is going to happen next.

The tall leader of the rustlers, whom they called Mack, came forward now with a big Western saddle. These saddles weighed at least forty pounds. Some had one cinch, others had two. The saddle which the leader carried had two cinches. He stepped slowly towards Tiger, talking quietly as he walked. Tiger did not move, but kept his head up and continued to flick his ears backwards and forwards.

One of the men called out to the leader, " Be careful, Mack! He might kick you! " Mack did not reply. He walked forward slowly until he stood beside Tiger, while the ropes on either side were held taut by the men. Then Mack lifted the saddle and dropped it on Tiger's back.

The big black horse flinched when he felt the saddle drop on his back, but after that he stood still again. Mack was afraid to reach under Tiger to get the rings of the cinches, so he called for a stick. One of the other rustlers got a long slender stick and handed it to Mack, who slowly reached under Tiger, got the ring for the front cinch, pulled it towards him, and then drew the cinch up very tight with the strap that was there for that purpose. A horse does not mind the single front cinch even when it is tight, for it pulls on his chest. The hind cinch, however, pulls on a horse's soft belly and is very uncomfortable. When this rear cinch was being drawn up tight, Tiger plunged and fought and tried to get away, but the four men grasping the ropes were too strong for him.

Ordinarily, a horse, even if he is a bucker, is ridden with only a halter, or hackamore, on his head. Now, however, one of the rustlers brought up a bridle with what was known as a curb bit. These steel curb bits could hurt a horse cruelly if the rider pulled hard on the bridle reins. When a man did that, the sharply curved bit sometimes cut the top of the horse's mouth until it bled.

When the bearded leader of the rustlers was satisfied that the saddle cinches were secure, he took the curb bit in his hand and slowly approached Tiger from the side, coming up close to his head. Now he intended to get the iron bit in Tiger's mouth.

During the months when Tiger had lived at the Sheridan Ranch, Jim had broken him to a bridle with a harmless link, or broken bit. Tiger had learned to open his mouth for Jim when he felt the bit against his teeth. Now the big rustler put the steel curb bit between Tiger's lips and pressed against his teeth a little, holding the bridle high and taut. Tiger opened his mouth. Mack quickly slipped the bit in Tiger's mouth and put the bridle over his ears.

" Who wants to try him? " asked Mack, looking around.

" You try him, Mack," several of the men said at the same time.

" All right," said the leader, " but hold on to the ropes. He's big and he's fast. We don't want him to get away."

Cowboys sometimes blindfold an unknown horse whom they believe to be dangerous, before trying to ride him. But this was not done to Tiger. The tall leader gathered the reins in one hand. He slowly put a foot in the stirrup, grasped the saddle horn, and, in a twinkling, mounted. Like all the other rustlers, he was wearing spurs with cutting wheels. To the surprise of all the men, Tiger at first made no move at all. He flinched when the man swung up on his back, but then stood still.

In those days it was unheard of for a rider to mount a horse without spurs. In order to break a horse to ride, most cowboys thought the rider needed both spurs and whip to subdue him. Mack had the usual quirt, or small whip, dangling from a leather loop on his right wrist and he wore a pair of heavy cutting spurs.

"Maybe he's gentle, Mack," one of the men called out. Another, standing in the rear, said, " I bet he's not. He looks like a wild cat to me."

The sun had come up in the east and shone on the scene where, for a moment, all was still. A Western lark flew down to the spring, dipped its bill in the water, and flew away. High above in the blue sky two hawks soared on silent wings.

The tall leader of the rustlers sat on Tiger and told the men holding the ropes to let them slacken. He did this in order to find out whether Tiger was tame and would make no trouble, or whether he had to be broken for riding. He must be made to move forward before this could be discovered.

When the ropes fell slack, Mack touched Tiger's flanks with the sharp spurs. The black horse leaped forward so quickly that he almost unseated his rider, but the man recovered himself and began to gouge Tiger's flanks hard with the sharp spurs. At the same time he struck him on the shoulder with the whip. Tiger did what was natural for him. He began bucking so hard that he quickly threw the rider and threw him hard. The four men held the ropes all the while but kept them slack in order to find out what Tiger might do. The tall man picked himself up from the ground and brushed the dust off his clothes. " This horse will bring a big price," he said, " and we're going to break him. The rest of you try him. He'll get tired after he's had enough of it."

The next man had no sooner mounted than Tiger dropped his shoulders a little, lurching sidewise at the same time, then whirled and leaped in the opposite direction so quickly that the rider was thrown even more violently than Mack had been.

Now the hard battle to subdue Tiger had begun. He was already breathing rapidly from his exertion and from the pain the riders had given him.

The third man had difficulty even in getting into the saddle, for Tiger knew now what was coming. He leaped and plunged, but the four men restraining him by the ropes made it possible for the rider to mount him. This man instantly jerked hard on the curb bit, trying to keep Tiger's head up. If this is accomplished, a horse has great difficulty in bucking. But in spite of the pain from the cutting bit, Tiger put his head down and again he used all his great strength in an effort to throw the man. Time after time the man jerked hard on the cruel bit, but Tiger endured the pain. He thrust his head down, plunging and bucking until he had thrown the rider. Then he stood, with wide, blazing eyes, looking at the other rustlers. Blood was trickling from Tiger's mouth where the curb bit had cut him. Because of his pain and fear, sweat was coming out all over his flanks.

The men were still sure that if they kept at it long enough, they would get the horse so tired he could not buck. Then, they thought, one of them would mount him and spur him into a gallop until he was exhausted. After that the great black horse would be broken and would obey his rider's commands. But Tiger's endurance, as well as his ability to stand punishment, amazed them. By means of his strength and his savage bucking, he continued to throw every man who got on his back, no matter how much he used the whip and the spurs.

Tiger stood, with sweat and foam on his sides, breathing hard yet showing by his flashing eyes that, although he had suffered, he was still full of fight.

The boss of the rustlers was even more interested in the great black horse than he had been at first. He knew now that Tiger had tremendous endurance as well as beauty, and he felt sure he could be sold for a price several times the amount paid for an ordinary horse.

Because Tiger was young and in fine condition, his strength and his determination to fight these men flowed back when they gave him even a few moments of rest. They did not realise this, since they were accustomed to average horses, who buck for a short while and then grow tired. Texas Pete and Bill had been eating breakfast while the others were trying to ride Black Tiger. Now, as the men stood arguing about which one should make the next try, Pete and Bill came up and joined the group. " All right, Pete," said the leader of the rustlers. " It's your turn. He's had so much you should be able to stay on him now."

The men holding the long ropes had let them

slacken until they both lay loose on the ground. Tiger stood so quietly that the ropes no longer seemed to be needed. He was breathing heavily. The men thought he might be too tired to buck again.

Pete moved slowly towards him until he got a hand on the saddle horn. Tiger jerked his head up and snorted. Pete leaped up in the saddle and at the same time kicked with his boots, causing the spurs to cut Tiger on both sides. The big horse leaped in the air and began bucking violently. Suddenly he jumped straight up with all four feet off the ground and came down hard with his feet close together. At the same instant he lunged sideways. Pete, who had already been severely jarred and jolted, now lost his balance entirely and he was thrown to the ground.

Suddenly Tiger gave way to all the fury roused in him by the cruel treatment he had received. His sides were bleeding where the sharp spurs had gouged him, and blood flowed from his mouth where it had been cut by the curb bit. He had paid no attention to the other riders after he threw them, but the instant Pete struck the ground, Tiger, his ears laid back, his long teeth gleaming, rushed for the man. Two of the rustlers dashed up and seized Pete by the feet to drag him out of danger. Tiger got his teeth in Pete's shoulder and struck at him with a front hoof. But the two men dragged their comrade away and Tiger could not follow, because the men holding the ropes suddenly drew them taut so that the big horse was stopped by the pull on both sides of his neck.

Pete got to his feet and stood back a distance, feeling his shoulder.

The boss said, " Well, it's a good thing for you the fellers helped you. It kinda looked like that horse was going to make buzzard feed out of you."

Pete scowled and said, " He's no good! Shoot him! "

Mack turned and stared at Pete. " Shoot, nothing! You harm that horse, and I'll shoot you! He's a great horse. We'll quit trying to tame him. We'll lead him—a feller with a rope on each side and a feller behind to keep him on the go. I'll get a big price for him."

Tiger was tied to a tree near the spot where he had thrown the men. The saddle and bridle were taken off and he was allowed to stand awhile before he was given a drink. Then he was taken to the spring, where he took long draughts of the clear cold water. When he had had enough he felt a new sense of comfort, except that he was hungry.

Slowly and watchfully, the men led Tiger away from the spring and down on the low level ground. Here they tied the ends of the long ropes to a tree so that he could reach plenty of grass. Tiger began grazing hungrily and no more attention was paid to him by any of the men. The main herd was being grazed farther down the valley under the watchful eyes of some of the men on horseback.

When Tiger raised his head, he could see the other horses grazing far down the valley. Once he looked towards the place where the horse rustlers were standing and talking over their plans for the coming night. But he did not take a second look. He knew they had him in their power for the time being, but if he got the least chance, he would try to escape.

CHAPTER SEVEN

ESCAPE

AT LAST the shadows of night began to fall. Tiger had eaten most of the grass in the space that the long ropes permitted him to reach, and he was no longer hungry or thirsty. The wounds in his mouth and sides were uncomfortable, though no longer actually painful. But Tiger was uneasy and restless. What he wanted above all else was to get away from these men whom he feared and hated.

When night came, with both moon and stars shining, the band of horse thieves broke up their camp and prepared to move. Mack, the leader of the rustlers, mounted his horse and rode over close to Tiger. Horse thief though he was, this man had a real feeling for a fine horse and he knew this big black fellow was as splendid a specimen as he had ever seen. He dismounted, led his horse up to

Tiger, and held out a piece of bread left over from the evening meal, knowing that some horses will eat bread. He talked quietly and came up slowly, leading his horse, so that Tiger was curious, especially when he smelled the bread being held out to him. He reached out his head towards the piece of bread but drew back without touching it. He was not in a mood to trust any of these men.

Still working quietly, the leader tied a much shorter rope around Tiger's neck and called to another rider to come up. When he did so, the boss said, " Here, Bill, take a half hitch of this rope around your saddle horn. You can lead this horse that way. I don't want to lead him by a long rope on his neck, so I'll take the long ones off. We may have to run to-night. If we do, we don't want to take a chance on getting tangled up in long ropes."

Bill did as he was ordered. After he had taken the two long ropes from Tiger's neck, he took not one but two turns of the shorter rope around his saddle horn and started slowly away.

When Tiger felt the first pull on his neck, he stood still. But as the rope continued to pull steadily, Tiger started forward and began to follow the man on the horse. His distrust of these men and everything they did was as strong as ever, but he would not show his hatred of them as long as they did not hurt him. So now he followed along obediently, ready every instant, however, to seize the slightest chance to escape.

The herd of horses was driven down the valley towards the east. They were started at a trot and the riders behind kept them moving forward. A man who was riding near Tiger reached over and tapped him on the hip with his hand when the horses were started. Tiger saw what was wanted and began trotting close to the horseman holding the rope.

The rustlers drove the horses at a trot for miles down the valley. Two men rode on each side of the herd to keep them bunched together as they trotted along. The horses were all much smaller than Tiger and they were of various colours, mostly dun colour, black, or brown; but among the others were two snow-white horses trotting with the stolen herd. These two white horses were only of average size, but they had been especially prized by the ranchman who had owned them.

It happened that when Alec McDowell, the

ranchman who owned the white horses, had discovered several days before that they had disappeared together with several others, he and another ranchman, Bud Maloney, decided to ride out at night and lie in hiding with their rifles, hoping to catch the thieves. Several nights had passed with no results. But, knowing that most stolen horses were driven eastward, Alec and Bud had, on this night, tied their horses behind a bluff and hidden themselves under a jutting ledge of rock facing the very trail over which the stolen horses were now being driven.

Tiger trotted along near the man who held the rope on his saddle horn. He did not know what the men intended to do with him, but the steady trotting pleased him, for he had an instinctive feeling that if he was moving along he might somehow escape. He trotted with his head up, looking all around him in the bright moonlight. He saw the herd of horses ahead of him, with the riders on each side. He paid no attention to the man holding the rope. The horseman riding behind him was careful not to ride too close to Tiger's heels. Knowing what a fighter he was, he did not want to stir him up.

When they had gone a considerable distance, Tiger saw the horseman on his right gallop up alongside the herd. Another horseman galloped behind him and a third man also followed the other two. They turned the horses towards the left and soon they were all moving on a trail leading up the hill towards the high land. They slowed to a walk as they went up the trail. Now and then Tiger's mouth hurt where the steel curb bit had wounded him, and then he passed his tongue over his lips. That was all he could do. His sides also stung from the sharp jabs of the cutting spurs, but his mind was only slightly on these discomforts. His main thought was directed to getting away from these men.

When all the horses had reached the high land, they were driven at a trot again. The horseman leading Tiger started his horse at a trot and as soon as Tiger felt the pull of the rope, he at once broke into a trot and kept alongside. He looked eagerly ahead at the moonlit high land, knowing that he was being held securely but ready at any time to run away if he was given the least chance.

For a while, as they travelled on, the high land

was mostly level and covered with the short buffalo grass, but now and then they came to a rocky stretch where the rains had washed away the top-soil. The herd of horses trotting across such places made loud, clattering sounds with their hoofs, and the horse rustlers did not like this. They knew it was always possible that ranchmen might be waiting to detect one of these stealthy night drives with the intention of recovering their stolen horses. The rustlers wished to make as little sound as possible.

The horses were kept at a trot for many miles across the high land. Then they came to a place where the land dipped down in a swag, or hollow, on the right side of which rose a low bluff with many ledges of rock jutting from the hillside.

Alec and Bud were hiding in the deep shadow of one of these ledges, and now in the bright moonlight they saw the horses coming at a trot down in the swag. At once Alec McDowell saw his two white horses trotting a little to one side of the herd.

Tiger, unaware of all that was going on in the minds of the horse rustlers and equally unaware of the two ranchmen hidden with their rifles in the shadows under the ledge, trotted down the incline and on to the level ground of the swag.

At the moment the horse rustlers were well separated. When they started down in the swag, all of them, including the man leading Tiger, were riding in single file on the side away from the rocky ledge, in order to make all the horses turn when they reached the low place. So the herd of horses was between the rustlers and the hidden ranchmen.

Nevertheless, this was the ranchmen's best chance. Suddenly, streaks of fire flashed from the shadows of the ledge and pandemonium broke loose both in the herd of horses and among the rustlers. The ranchmen were firing across the herd of horses at the thieves. At the first rifle shot, the rustlers ducked down low on their horses, wheeled them about, and spurred them at a gallop back towards the west. The man who was leading Tiger also ducked low, threw the end of Tiger's rope from his saddle horn, and spurred his horse at a gallop after the other rustlers.

Tiger ran free, frightened by the sound of the shots and the flashes of fire. He ran with the other horses and, because he was both free and frightened, he leaped on at full speed and soon passed the others and left them all far behind. The rope on his neck was not long. It dangled a foot above the ground. There was a knot in the end that now and then bounced back and struck him on the leg, but this did not lessen his speed.

Tiger did not know that all the rustlers had escaped and that the two ranchmen had mounted their horses and were following the herd. When daylight came, they would round up their own horses and take them back. He knew only that he was wholly free again from the men who had tormented him. He did not feel any longer the sting in his mouth from the steel curb bit or the wounds in his sides from the cutting spurs. His mind was filled with the thrilling sense of liberty. With this new feeling he ran on and on and on.

However, when he had covered miles on the high land which he reached when he ran up the incline from the swag, he began to have an almost pleasant sense of weariness. At last he slowed to a trot, and a little later to a walk.

When he came to a place where the high ground ended, he stopped and stood on the border of the shadowy land beyond. The ground ahead dipped down and was filled with many thick growths of low trees and bushes, with here and there open grassy places. Tiger stood for a time on the edge of the high ground and looked at the clusters of trees and bushes, all standing silent, dark, and lonely in the strange wild land. The rope, of which he was hardly aware, dangled from his neck. His main concern was to be certain there were no men anywhere near him. He stood a long time, breathing deeply from his long run and looking at the place in front of him. Once he turned and looked back across the high land. He thought of the men. But he saw nothing but the silent prairie with the moonlight shining upon it.

As Tiger stood in the open on the higher ground, he dropped his head to rest, after the manner of a weary horse. He felt safe enough for the time, so his head sank lower and lower and he fell into a fitful doze.

Suddenly a smell came to Tiger that made him jerk his head up quickly. He saw a big timber wolf standing in an open space below. Tiger snorted loudly, and angrily stamped a big front hoof on the ground. The timber wolf took one quick look, then slunk out of sight in some bushes.

Tiger felt that it would be safer farther away from the low land with its hiding places for the wolf and others of its kind. He turned about and walked across the level ground towards a small hill in the distance. Then he walked up to the top of this hill and looked around him in every direction. He saw nothing but the silent buffalo grass reaching as far as he could see. Standing in the lonely night, he heard, far away towards the north, sounds that made him curious. He stood with his head up, looking in that direction.

What he heard was the barking of a lone dog. The night was so still that the sound of the barking came to him even though the dog was a long distance away. Tiger did not know that off in that direction there was a ranch-house with many men, all asleep at this hour of the night.

Listening, Tiger looked in wonderment for a time towards the distant barking, the only sound to break the stillness of the night. He remained on the little hill, awake and alert, until the grey dawn appeared. Then, feeling hungry, he began to graze on the grass which was everywhere around him.

Every now and then when he put his head down to graze, he stepped on the rope and it bothered him. But he was able to eat in spite of that. Fortunately, when he held his head up, the rope swung clear of the ground and could not trip him.

When sunrise came, the men of the Bar Z cattle ranch, where the dog had been barking, were all out in the yard saddling their horses for the day's riding on the open range. The ranch-house, corrals, and stables were well up on high ground, with a very high ridge just west of the buildings.

It happened that the owner of the ranch, Lloyd McBain, looked off in the direction where at the moment Tiger was standing again on the high knoll. Instantly McBain was much interested. He called to his foreman, John West, and said, " Come here and look at this new horse! "

John came up to the place where McBain stood, and looked where he pointed. " Well," exclaimed John, " that's a beauty. There's a horse that's a fine one. I wonder if we could get him and see if there's a brand on him."

" Tell the men," said McBain. " We'll try for him. If we can get him to run towards that cut in the hills at Wild Horse Springs, we'll have a good chance to rope him."

When the great black horse in the distance was pointed out to the other men, all of them were at once eager for the chase.

Tiger, in the meantime, had been looking towards the men and horses he saw moving there far away across the range. As he looked, there came to him the memory of his home on the ranch with Jim and the other men. But he was in strange surroundings now and, after his recent experience, he was afraid of all strange men.

While Tiger stood looking, he saw the men on their horses ride directly away from him, cross over a ridge, and disappear. Tiger looked towards the distant ridge for a few minutes, wondering if he would see any more men appear there. He saw nothing but the lonely ridge, with one tall cedar tree growing on the summit. He snorted once, both curious and a little apprehensive at the sight of so many mounted men. Then he looked at the distant ranch buildings, but the place seemed deserted now. Not a horse or a man moved anywhere near it. He walked down the knoll and trotted off towards the south, directly away from the ranch. It seemed to him that he should get right away from the place.

He soon came to a point where the high ground dipped down to the narrow valley of the Big Sandy River. He walked down the steep hill and came to the level valley. The green grass grew all along it and, feeling hungry, he began to graze.

After Tiger had grazed up along the valley for quite a while, he raised his head to look back and was startled to see a number of men on horses coming out of a cut in the hill behind him. They were coming towards him, well separated from each other, with their horses moving at a walk. At once Tiger was frightened. He snorted loudly. With head and tail raised, he trotted around in a big circle, stopping to look intently at the oncoming riders. Then he made up his mind.

He snorted again, whirled in the opposite direction, and galloped away towards the west. But the riders held their horses to a walk. Tiger did not run far, because when he turned to look he saw the horses were still walking.

" John, look at him! " said McBain. " He's the finest horse I ever saw."

"He is that," said John, "and he's likely to outrun us all unless we can keep him headed towards the trap."

Tiger had not seen what the men had done when they vanished from his sight behind the ridge beyond the ranch buildings. At McBain's order, three riders went off at a gallop away from the other men. They rode up and over a ridge, and then on behind it until they reached a cut in the ridge known as Wild Horse Springs. They planned to hide there in some clumps of trees and surprise Tiger if he tried to escape through the cut.

The Big Sandy River curved in near a very steep hill at this place where the men planned to hide, and the space between the hill and the river was very narrow. The three men intended to leap suddenly out from the trees as Tiger approached, and they believed that their sudden appearance would frighten him so badly that he would whirl and run back towards the other men. If he did that it seemed certain that one or more of these skilled riders could throw a loop over his head.

The other men did not ride hard after Tiger, because they wanted to give the three riders time to get in position, hidden in the trees in the narrow cut.

In July and August, the Big Sandy River generally flowed broad but very shallow. However, heavy rains sometimes turned it into a deep, rushing flood. The river was flooded at this time, so the men felt certain Tiger would not whirl and leap into the water. Moreover, the high sandy bank on this side was very steep and the main current of the river flowed near it. The three riders knew that if Tiger leaped into the river here he would have to leap off this high bank into the flood, and all of them believed that this was a feat no horse would dare to attempt. They knew horses and their habits, but most of the horses they had known were the average kind.

The other men, now walking their horses behind Tiger, knew by his long legs and graceful build that it was unlikely they could ever run him down on open land. But they believed their plan would work. If he ran back and tried to break through them, he would have to run so close that one of them could surely throw a loop over his head and catch him.

After some time had passed and McBain felt

sure that the three men were in position, he gave
the order to gallop fast after Tiger and so make
him extend himself. He would then be all the
more frightened when the three riders suddenly
rode out into the narrow space between himself
and the river. It seemed certain that he would
whirl about when the three riders rode out and
blocked him, and would try to rush back past
the other men.

The oncoming riders were a little spread out
as they galloped their horses behind Tiger. He
now found himself running along the base of
the high, steep hill on his right, with the flooded
river not far away on his left. He had not yet
run as fast as he could, but as the men pursued
him on their horses, he began to run more
swiftly.

On and on Tiger ran, keeping a good distance
between himself and the horsemen. The way ahead
looked clear to him. He had no desire to turn
towards the high, steep hill on his right and leap
up that sharp slope. It seemed to him he could
escape by staying in the open valley between the
river and the steep hill.

The men behind Tiger now put their horses at

a swift gallop, but Tiger ran on, thinking he surely could escape up the valley. There were more than twenty mounted men behind him. The sounds of the many hoofs striking the sod came to Tiger's ears and he was alarmed by the very number of the men and horses.

The green valley lay silent in the clear sunlight, and presently Tiger came in sight of the grove of trees between himself and the cut in the hill. He saw nothing to fear in them and there was no wind to warn him of the hidden riders. At that point the river curved in close to the grove of trees.

Tiger raced on, with the many riders coming along behind him. He was coming near the grove of trees now, with the river close at his left.

Then it happened. The three hidden riders, cleverly gauging the distance, suddenly rode out from the grove of trees, yelling and firing their big six-shooters. Tiger came to a sudden halt, whirled on the instant, and ran back.

The riders coming behind thought to themselves, Now we'll get him!

Then Tiger saw that he was trapped. He faced the many riders. The three men near the grove still kept yelling and firing their revolvers. At an order from McBain, all the horsemen stopped. He called out to the men, " Be careful! We'll have a good chance if he tries to break through. Every man have his loop ready. If he comes, he'll come hard! "

Tiger stood for a moment, breathing heavily and looking with wide, frightened eyes at the men. Then the big black horse rushed for the river bank, while the men spurred their mounts and began to whirl their lassos to rope him. He had moved so fast and so unexpectedly that only one rope touched him and that fell harmlessly on his back.

He came to the edge of the high bank, and without a second's pause he leaped far out into the dark, swollen flood. The men pulled up their horses at the edge. They were amazed that any horse should have attempted such a jump and disappointed at the failure of their plans.

Tiger went clear under the water. Then he came up, his black head showing as he swam, while the rushing water carried him downstream.

At the suggestion of McBain, the men galloped down the stream along the bank. Then they pulled up their horses and looked back. Tiger was swimming steadily at an angle and crossing the river as it carried him down. Once, when his head sank lower, McBain said, " Now I hope he gets across. It would be a shame for a fine horse like that to drown."

Tiger fought on to reach the other side, gaining slowly but steadily. As he neared the other shore, his head seemed to sink lower. At last his feet touched the bottom. He pushed up out of the water and stood on the long, sloping bank, his head lowered, gasping for breath. His black, flowing mane and tail hung like rags, with the water streaming from them to the ground.

After a while Tiger raised his head and looked across at the many mounted men. There was no fire in his eyes now, only a look of weariness and suffering. He turned and walked very slowly towards some willow trees near the stream and stepped under their low-hanging branches so that he was concealed from the men on the other side of the river. He stood there for a while to get his breath and then walked on and up to an open grassy valley.

Far ahead of him he saw a long line of trees

reaching out across the valley. He walked with his head low, reached the woods, and moved in towards a small stream murmuring over its sandy bed. Here he drank, rested, and drank again. Then, feeling he was safe from the men now, he lay down to rest. All was quiet in the shady woods around him.

CHAPTER EIGHT

THE WILD HERD

IN THE next week Tiger wandered for many miles, grazing by day and stopping for the night, generally on wide open land where no dangerous enemy could be concealed. He felt lonely, especially in the long, dark hours of the night, when he would doze with his head down and then would quickly raise it to watch for riders who might be pursuing him. He had no aim except to find plenty of grass to eat in the daytime and clear water to drink when he was thirsty.

Early one morning, after a week had passed since he jumped into the river to escape from McBain and his men, Tiger was standing on open ground and looking towards the west. Not far away he saw a long fringe of trees and, knowing there were often streams in such places, he walked into the woods. Sure enough, there was a small stream, bordered on each side by a gravelly bank covered with small flat rocks. Tiger walked over the rocks and stepped into the water, which came about half-way to his knees. Just as he finished drinking, he heard the clattering of horses' hoofs on the rocky bank of the stream, just around a sharp bend. He also heard one or two horses squeal, as horses sometimes do when they draw near to each other as they are about to drink.

Tiger was curious about these horses and he was also apprehensive, thinking that there might be men with them. He walked into the water and crossed the shallow stream to the other side. Now he could see that there were no men with the horses.

A herd of about twenty wild horses had come to drink from the stream. Some of the horses were larger than the average wild horse and unusually well built. The leader was a stallion, bright bay in colour, and he was larger than any of the others, weighing about eleven hundred pounds. At this time Tiger himself weighed about thirteen hundred pounds.

The instant the wild bay stallion saw Tiger, he lifted his head high, uttered a loud snort of

defiance, and came walking downstream through
the creek towards Tiger.

Tiger stood his ground at the edge of the stream
with only his front hoofs in the water. He did not
move back but stood waiting. The bay horse
walked over the rocky rapids in the stream and came
on. Seeing that Tiger did not run, the stallion laid
back his ears and, with teeth showing, charged
through the water at the black horse.

Tiger whirled and slammed his hoofs back,
turning so quickly that one hoof caught the
stallion hard on the side of the head before he
could jump away. For an instant the big bay was
bewildered by the shock of the blow. He held his
head up and blinked his eyes rapidly as a horse
does when he receives a hard blow on the head.
After kicking, Tiger whirled about again and, with
his ears laid back like a fighting dog, he charged
the stallion, who turned to run. Tiger bit him and
pursued him.

The bay horse, with Tiger after him, ran up
the shallow stream to a point opposite the other
wild horses, who stood on the bank, watching
what was happening. Tiger stopped and looked at
them. The stallion snorted loudly, then leaped

away to the open ground. His snort was a signal to the others to follow. They took a good look at the big black horse standing watching them; then with one accord they all splashed across the stream and followed the lead of the wild stallion across the open land.

A gelding does not often fight a stallion unless he is cornered. But occasionally a gelding is a real fighter, and then he will not only challenge a stallion but will continue to fight as long as he has any strength left in him. Tiger was that unusual kind of horse.

As the wild horses came out on the open grassland, Tiger followed them. He was lonely and wanted to be with other horses. When the bay stallion gave another snort and began galloping, the herd followed him and Tiger also moved along behind at a gallop.

It happened that some riders of the range had seen these wild horses when they entered the woods along the stream and passed out of sight. They had come up over a hill just in time to see the herd disappear among the trees. The men knew the horses had gone into the woods to drink from the stream. At first they did not see Tiger because

he had disappeared in the woods before they were
near enough to see him. However, a moment later
the men, through an opening in the trees, got a
glimpse of the great black horse standing with his
head high, looking upstream. Then they saw the
bay stallion charge forward to attack him, and they
watched Tiger whirl and kick the horse and then
whirl again and go for him with his teeth. In a
twinkling the bay stallion came bursting out of the
woods, and he and the rest of the wild horses went
galloping off across the plain with Tiger galloping
behind them.

These riders saw that Tiger was a most magnificent horse. They believed he would be a great
saddle horse if only they could capture him. They
had had their eyes on this particular herd of wild
horses for some time, because there were some
unusual and valuable specimens among them. They
wanted the best of the lot to break for saddle
horses, and they were eager to capture the bay
stallion if they could ever get a rope over his head.
Now, however, they wanted the great black horse
galloping behind the wild herd much more than
any of the others. They knew all the horses over a
wide range and saw that he was a stranger. He

would be the property of anyone fortunate enough to capture him.

The riders held a hurried consultation. They knew that the horses were galloping in the direction of a box canyon. The country was broken by two ridges that rose between the canyon and the plain where the herd was running. If the wild horses, with the big black horse following, ran in the right direction, the men thought they might be able to ride over the ridges behind the herd and perhaps make Tiger run into the canyon, where he would soon come to its dead end. If he tried to run back past the men, they thought one or more might be able to rope him.

The wild herd, with Tiger close behind, galloped on over the prairie and passed in between the two ridges. The men knew the place well. There was unusually good grass not far from the canyon, and they hoped the wild horses would lead Tiger to this grazing ground. If the herd stopped to feed there on the low ground, the big black horse might graze near them. Then there might be a chance for the men, by keeping out of sight behind the ridges, to ride down from both sides swiftly and confuse the black horse by yelling and shooting their revolvers so that he would run for the box canyon.

The men knew they had not been seen, because of the fearless way the wild horses galloped. They also knew that when the horses stopped, one of them would act as a lookout and keep watch for riders or any other danger while the rest of the herd grazed. An old mare often stood guard for a herd of wild horses, apparently making an even better lookout than the stallion that led them.

The herd galloped on steadily in the direction of the canyon and passed out of sight in the distance, where there were many low dips, bushes, and clumps of trees in the rough land. The big black horse was still following them.

After skilful planning to prevent any scent or other warning from reaching the wild horses, the men finally got into position on both ridges so that they could peep down at the herd. The wild horses and Tiger were grazing on the low ground, and one of the horses had slowly started to climb the eastern ridge. This was the old lookout mare. The ridge was so steep that she could not go up quickly, but once she had gained the top she would surely see the men hiding there.

The riders on both sides acted instantly. They

spurred out of their hiding places and raced down the ridges behind the wild horses. They did this so swiftly that they were quite near before the wild herd and Tiger saw them. The stallion threw up his head, whirled, and started running towards the canyon, and all the others followed. Now the men began to yell at the top of their voices and fire their six-shooters, hoping to keep the horses running all the way into the canyon. The bay stallion, however, was suspicious. He whirled again and leaped up the high ridge where the old mare was now standing. Two horses followed him, but the others, in their fright at all the yelling and and shooting, ran straight ahead on the low land.

Tiger ran also, but he stayed behind the others. When he saw the walls of the canyon ahead, he knew that this was a trap. He stopped and looked at the hard-riding men coming on towards him. They yelled louder and fired into the ground near him, trying to keep him running with the others. Now that they had had a good look at Tiger, they cared nothing for the remainder of the herd.

The black horse took one quick glance at the high ridges on each side. He realised that it would be slow going up those steep places, while the land between him and the men was all level. Paying no attention to the bullets kicking up dirt around him, he leaped with a mighty burst of speed directly towards the oncoming riders. He saw only one gap between them and he rushed for it. The men tried desperately to close the space and one man succeeded in getting directly in front of Tiger as the others dashed in swiftly from both sides. They crowded him so hard that he did not turn towards either side but continued straight ahead. The rider directly in front of him cast his loop when Tiger was almost upon him, but the rope missed. Tiger, scarcely checking his speed, crashed into the smaller horse, knocking down both horse and rider. Then he leaped past them all and ran free.

The men pursued him for a little way, but they soon saw it was no use and pulled to a stop. The fallen man and his horse got up and stood gazing after Tiger as he raced away. He shot like a black meteor down the level land at a speed that amazed the men. They saw him gallop on and on until he was only a black speck in the distance.

CHAPTER NINE

TIGER SAVES A LIFE

BY THIS time Jim Summers had decided that he would never see Tiger again. For months after that night when Old Snorter broke out of the corral and disappeared with him, Jim rode far and wide, hoping to see or hear something of his young black horse. At the end of a year Jim had only a dim hope of recovering him, and when two years had passed it seemed impossible that Tiger would ever be found. Jim knew that any one of several things could have happened. Hungry wolves could have killed him in the dead of winter, or he might have been captured by horse thieves. Such thieves would have seen the John Sheridan brand on Tiger's shoulder, but that would not have troubled them. If they had wanted to, they could have blotted or changed the brand, but even that would not have been necessary. It would not have been difficult, in spite of the brand, to sell him to other dishonest men who would take him far away. Such things often happened in those days.

So Jim, having given up hope, was electrified by the news brought to him one evening. Buck Davis came galloping across the grass-covered plain and pulled his horse to a stop in the yard of the Sheridan ranch, where Jim and several other men were standing.

Buck said, " Jim, I think I've got good news for you. I saw a rider to-day who is in these parts looking for a bunch of strayed cattle. He says he saw a fine big black horse far over on a range to the west. He told me the boss and the whole outfit of riders there chased this big black one day. They ran all their horses down, but the horse put on speed when some men on fresh horses cut in and tried to catch him. When last seen, he was over in the Black Wolf Springs country. This fellow said that a gang of horse thieves had been over there a while back, but there was no sign of them lately. It's a good day's ride to the Springs. Night would catch you, but you could sleep on the grass and hunt again the next day. Of course," Buck added, " Tiger has been gone a good while. He might not remember you, even if you got close and called him."

" If that horse is Tiger, he'll know me," said Jim. " I was with him so much, I don't think he ever would forget me. I'll start as soon as it's daylight."

Several of the men offered to go with Jim, but he said he wanted to go alone to find Tiger. From everything Buck had told him, Jim was convinced that the horse the rider had seen was really Black Tiger. So the next morning Jim started off on his horse at dawn, carrying some dried beef which would be all he needed to eat. He rode one of the horses used regularly for range riding.

Jim rode on steadily at an easy gallop until he had gone about ten miles. Then he kept the horse at a jog trot for a while. He wanted to reach Black Wolf Springs by sunset, since he thought it just possible that Tiger might come there to drink if he really was in that neighbourhood. If that happened, Jim was determined to be near enough to call to him.

Jim made good time. He reached Black Wolf Springs more than an hour before sunset and let his horse have a drink. There were two springs at this place, close together at the base of a hill. All

around them were tall, leafy thickets and a little
west of them there was a growth of pine woods.

Jim knew his horse was tired and hungry after
the ride, so he led him to some green grass near
the pine woods. He put hobbles on the horse's
front feet so that he could not stray too far away.
Then he took off the saddle and bridle and removed
the rifle from its holster on the saddle. Jim also
had a revolver in his belt. He had no fear of the
horse thieves if they were still around. They would
not be apt to take chances with a cowboy, knowing
that he would be fully armed and alert for any
danger.

Jim walked a little distance from the woods and
found a sharp drop in the ground where he could
sit with his back against the low earth bank and
peep across at the springs. He put the rifle, bridle,
and saddle beside him and sat down on the soft
dry earth at the bottom of the bank. Jim felt
hungry, so he took some dried beef from the sack
on the saddle and sat munching it, with all his
thoughts on Tiger. He knew that the fine black
horse the men had chased might not be Tiger, but
he still felt there was a chance. Tiger had been a
two-year-old colt when he ran away with his

mother, and now, if he was still alive, he would be a great, full-grown four-year-old.

Would he remember me and the good days we had together? Jim wondered.

If the horse came to the springs and got his scent, Jim believed Tiger would be curious enough to come up close. Certainly the big black horse had been seen near these springs, so he must know that the clear, gushing water was here. And night was the time when the horse would be likely to come here if he was thirsty.

Jim untied the blanket on the rear of his saddle and wrapped it around him, for these nights were chill. He thought he would stay awake for a long time, on the chance that the black horse might come in the night to drink. The sky was clear and the stars were shining brightly.

Some time passed and Jim began to doze. Then he fell asleep, leaning back against the low bank. A gentle breeze blowing from the west stirred through the pine trees and made the branches of the leafy thickets sway gently, but with scarcely any sound.

Jim had been asleep only about an hour when a great black horse moved past some tall bushes near the foot of a hill and came out in the open, looking towards the springs. It was Black Tiger. At once he saw Jim's horse grazing on the open ground near the trees, but there was no saddle on him and he seemed to be quite free to do as he wished. Tiger stood for a time watching the horse and then walked past another thicket so that there was only open ground between him and the springs. He walked a little nearer, and all at once he flinched and stopped as though he had been struck. A scent had come to him that was like no other he had ever known. It was the scent of the only man whom Tiger in all his life had learned to love. He walked a little nearer and then saw Jim sitting in the shadows, leaning quietly back against the bank.

Although this was surely the scent of the one man Tiger trusted, he still held back. After all, he had taken severe punishment from men and had felt that he must never again let himself fall into their clutches. He looked towards the peacefully grazing horse. Then again he looked at the man leaning against the bank in the shadows. Tiger breathed a long breath ending like a sigh. Then he walked nearer. Yes, that was surely Jim's scent. Tiger put his head down to be nearer still. He took another step, then another. He could no longer keep still. With his head almost over Jim, he began to make low, friendly sounds.

Jim woke up with a start and could scarcely believe his eyes. The great black horse's nose was almost touching him. "Tiger!" he whispered. "Black Tiger!" Tiger touched his nose to Jim's head and again made soft sounds, trying in his own way to talk to him.

As Jim slowly got to his feet, he kept calling the horse by name. Then he reached up and put his hands on Tiger's head. "You didn't forget. You can't tell how you found me, but I know you got my scent. Now," said Jim, the thought suddenly coming to him, "I'm going to put the saddle and bridle on you and ride you home. I know we'll be friends just as we were before."

Jim brought the saddle, lifted it up, gently placed it on Tiger's back, and tightened the cinches. He did not put the bridle on yet. Instead, he said, "Tiger, I wonder if you've had a drink. Come with me and I'll see." Jim took hold of the short rope which was still on Tiger's neck and walked to the springs with the horse following him very closely. There Tiger put his nose down to the water and drank for some time. Then Jim put the bridle on and led Tiger to the other horse and took off the hobbles. He felt sure the horse would go home, since ranch horses always do if they are no more than a day's journey away.

Jim wondered a little if Tiger would object to being ridden. He put his foot in the stirrup, swung up, and seated himself. Patting Tiger on the shoulder, he touched him gently with the heels of his boots, and said, " Let's go, Tiger! " At once the black horse started down the valley at a fast walk and then, of his own accord, he broke into a gallop and moved with long, easy strides across the land.

When the other horse saw Jim riding off down the valley on Tiger, he did not want to be left alone, so he set out after them at a fast gallop, eager to get back to the horses at the ranch. He ran even faster than Tiger, but the black horse only pricked up his ears when the other horse passed him, and held to the gallop at which he had started.

Soon the moon came up and cast a brighter light over the land. After riding for a while Jim felt that the cinch of the saddle was a little loose. He had not wanted to make it too tight at first. He pulled gently on the reins and said, " Let's stop, Tiger."

The black horse understood the pull on the reins and came to a stop. Jim dismounted and tightened the cinch a little, patted Tiger affectionately, and said, " There now, Tiger! We won't be bothered with that again."

Nothing in all these lonely years had given Tiger such joy as he now felt at the touch of Jim's hand and the soft, friendly sounds of his voice. He was the kind of horse that would always appreciate and respond to affection just as he would fight any man who gave him hard treatment.

At last Jim knew he was more than half-way home. He rode down from a stretch of high ground into a long valley filled with bushes and trees. Tiger slowed to a walk and pricked up his ears; then he turned and walked up to a spring and began to drink.

Jim dismounted and waited. Tiger raised his head, turned about, and immediately began to eat grass hungrily. " Well, Tiger," said Jim. " I forgot you might be hungry. You've been chased so much, I guess you do most of your grazing at night." Jim removed the bridle and took the blanket down from the back of the saddle. "You go on and eat, Tiger," he said. "I'll lie down a little while. We're more than half-way home. Eat all the grass you want."

Jim did not take the rifle from its holster on the saddle, thinking there was no need for it. He went a short distance away and lay down on the level ground with his blanket rolled about him. He soon went to sleep, knowing that Tiger would not leave him.

It happened that three of the gang of horse thieves who had previously captured Tiger were riding in the direction of the John Sheridan Ranch. They hoped to find some range horses far enough from the ranch-house that they could be driven away. They were well hidden by the many trees and tall bushes to the south when they first saw the lone rider on the big black horse, but they recognised Tiger at once. Here was another chance at the prize that had slipped through their fingers before. Keeping well back, so that no sounds would reach the rider's ears, they followed. They saw the black horse stop at the spring and saw the rider turn the horse loose to graze, while he himself lay down on the ground. At once they tied their own horses to some trees, and one of the three stayed close to them to prevent them from making any noise. They knew that one of their own horses might nicker when he saw the black horse. If one of the three horses should raise his head and look intently in Tiger's direction, the man would instantly clamp his hand over the horse's nose and distract his attention. But the horses belonging to the rustlers were very weary from the hard riding given them. When they were tied to the trees, they dropped their heads, wanting to do nothing but rest.

The other two thieves stole forward on foot until they could see Tiger in the moonlight. To their great satisfaction, they saw the butt of the rifle sticking up from its holster on the saddle. It did not occur to them that Jim might have a revolver in his belt. Each man had brought a coil of rope with him, and their plan was simple. They would sneak up from behind some tall bushes and throw both loops over Tiger's head before he had a chance to see them. Then, if the man awoke, they would tell him they would shoot if he got up or made a move towards the rifle. The only reason they were reluctant to kill a ranchman was that if they did so, they would have to leave that part of the country for good, and would have to travel far and fast if they succeeded in getting away. All the ranchmen would be after them. These horse thieves were carrying on what they thought of as a kind of business, and they used great caution and took no unnecessary risks. But horse thieves in those days were notorious for the way they often bungled their attempts at crime, and many of them were very poor shots.

That was how it happened that the thieves bungled their attempt to steal Tiger again. The two men dropped on all fours and came on behind the bushes like sneaking wolves, thinking that when they were close enough they would rush out and toss their loops over Tiger before he knew what they were up to.

Jim had been sleeping soundly, but he was awakened by a sudden noise in the bushes. He sat up and was amazed at what he saw. Tiger, with his ears back and his teeth bared, was charging towards a man hiding in the underbrush. Jim seized his pistol, but for a moment he had no chance to use it. He heard Tiger squeal with rage and saw him leap into the bushes. Then two men

men burst out of the thicket on the other side and dodged behind another clump of underbrush with Tiger close behind them. Jim fired three quick shots towards the two men, but he could not really aim at them, because Tiger was in the way.

At the sound of the shots Tiger stopped, threw up his head, and looked towards the place where Jim was crouching on the ground. Jim called to him loudly, " Tiger, Tiger, come here! "

With his head up, Tiger came back at a gallop Jim fired several other shots in the direction the men had run in, but he knew they were already out of range. As soon as Tiger came up, Jim mounted quickly, holding the bridle on his arm, and started at a run down the valley. He felt certain that the men were rustlers and knew it was possible that others might be concealed somewhere in the vicinity. The wisest move would be to get away as fast as possible.

Jim galloped Tiger for a long distance with no rest. Then he quickly dismounted, put the bridle on, mounted again, and galloped on once more. He was quite sure there was no longer any danger.

The men knew he was armed and alert, and he

was certain they would not follow him as far as this. But now Jim wanted to get home. He knew Tiger had great endurance and he let him continue at a gallop. Jim felt certain he would reach the ranch house some time late in the night.

After a while Jim let Tiger go along at his own gait, and he slowed down to a trot and then to a walk. When he had walked a little, he started out of his own accord at a gallop. He kept his head up, looking eagerly at the moonlit plain before him. Jim believed that Tiger knew he was on his way home and was as eager to get there as Jim himself.

Well along in the night they reached a valley that Jim knew was about five miles from the ranch house. Tiger trotted down the incline to the valley and turned into a cattle trail that led on past many bushes and small groves of trees. Then he broke into a canter and Jim let him have his way.

It happened that a big timber wolf was lying asleep in some bushes near the trail. The wolf had eaten heavily from a cow carcass not long before and was in a deep sleep after his gorge. If the wind had been blowing towards the wolf, its sense of smell might have awakened it. But there was scarcely a leaf moving.

Tiger was almost on top of the sleeping wolf before it woke. Then it jumped out of the bushes almost under the horse's heet. Tiger leaped violently to one side, and the limb of a tree struck Jim on the side of the head, knocking him out of the saddle to the ground. Jim was a good rider, but it all happened so quickly he had no chance to protect himself.

At first he was unconscious as he lay on the ground. Tiger stood close to him with his nose almost touching Jim's face, at the same time making soft sounds in an attempt to get some response. At last Jim sat up, although he was still dazed and not fully conscious, and then his head was close to the stirrup. Tiger stood perfectly still. Jim reached up and grasped the stirrup and tried to pull himself up by it, but the effort was too much. He lost consciousness again and fell back on the ground.

Dimly, Jim knew that he had fallen from Tiger's back and must keep trying to get in the saddle and ride again. He managed to get up on his hands and knees and clutch a stirrup with one hand.

But try as he would, he could not pull himself up on his feet. Into his dazed mind came the memory that once he had taught Tiger to kneel at command. Very weakly, he uttered the word, "Down!" For a moment the great black horse moved uneasily as if he did not understand. Then once more Jim said, " Down, Tiger," and slowly the horse lowered himself to the ground close beside Jim. Now it was possible for Jim to reach the saddle horn, and somehow he managed to pull himself along until he was in the saddle. He had no strength to say, " Up," but without the order from Jim, the big horse raised himself carefully and started walking forward.

It seemed to Tiger that he should go on, because that must be what Jim wanted him to do, although he gave him no orders. Tiger felt like breaking into a canter, but he did not do so, because Jim was acting in such a strange way. So it seemed to Tiger that he must keep on walking until Jim gave him some word.

The big black horse walked on across the level valley. He felt restless and, as the time passed, more and more uneasy about the change that had come over Jim. He did not know why Jim was so quiet. Jim said nothing and he did not move in the saddle at all, but sat perfectly still. Because of this, Tiger felt he must not break from a walk unless he was ordered to.

Jim had only just enough consciousness to be able to hold himself in the saddle. His head was bowed and his hands were clenched on the saddle horn. Only a man who had spent most of his life on horseback could have kept himself from sliding to the ground after such a blow on the head as Jim had received. But dazed and sick as he was, Jim automatically gripped Tiger's sides with his knees and clung to the saddle horn with both his hands. That was all he was able to do. The bridle reins hung loose on Tiger's neck. If they were to get back to John Sheridan's Ranch, the black horse would have to find his own way. Jim could do nothing now to guide him.

Tiger walked slowly on. A cool wind sprang up, and Tiger was filled with a growing feeling of anxiety. He could not understand why Jim kept him at this slow pace for such a long time. He did not once feel Jim's hand or hear him speak a single word. This had a strange effect on the horse, who somehow felt his own responsibility.

He must go on at a walk. That must be what Jim wanted him to do.

Presently they came to a deep, narrow ditch in the ground which Tiger could easily have jumped across. He stopped, waiting for Jim to gather up the reins and give him the signal to jump. When nothing happened, the horse turned his head back as far as he could and tried to touch Jim's leg with his nose. But Jim only sat silent in the saddle.

Tiger drew a long breath and uttered a low, anxious sound. Then he turned to his right and walked along the edge of the ditch until it ended near a hill about half a mile away. There he went around the head of the ditch on level ground, and once more turned back in the direction he had been following before. Although two years had passed since Tiger had been anywhere near this part of the country, it seemed familiar to him. Some instinct told him that he was headed for the ranch and that he must keep on walking until he got there. The big horse saw the line of hills on the right, the familiar small stream flowing out of the valley, and the tall trees near the stream. All these stirred dim memories in Tiger. Even the silent rocks on the nearby hillside looked familiar, for he was now in a place he had travelled over with Jim many times. But the rocks on the hillside, the tall trees, and all the valley lay in the strangest silence. The only sounds were Tiger's own steady hoofbeats as he walked over the prairie sod.

He stopped once more and turned his head back towards Jim, making low, friendly sounds. He could see Jim sitting slumped down in the saddle, with his head bowed. But Jim would not speak. He would only sit in the saddle with his head bowed down in silence.

A dark, threatening cloud was looming up in the west now, and the change in the air made Tiger more uneasy than ever. A thunderstorm was coming up, and he wanted to break into a gallop in order to reach shelter before the storm. Again he looked back anxiously at Jim, but there was no change. Jim neither moved nor spoke. Breathing out a long breath, Tiger walked on up the valley. He looked intently at all the country before him and became more and more eager. He was approaching the place he knew so well. He was not afraid to go there. It was the place where he had lived with Jim and the other men who had been kind to him.

The cloud in the west was coming up rapidly now, and Tiger heard the first roll of thunder. He knew the storm was close and he moved faster but still held to a walk.

Suddenly he rounded a turn in the valley and saw the ranch house, with the tall trees standing near it and the other trees not far from the stables. The buildings were all in silent darkness with no light to be seen anywhere.

John Sheridan lay asleep on his bunk by a window of the ranch house. He was awakened by the sound of hoofs on the ground just outside his window and then heard a horse making anxious nickering noises. The ranch horses were all in the corrals or out on the range, and Sheridan knew at once that something must be wrong. Jumping into his clothes, he seized a lantern, lit it, and rushed outside.

There in the beam from the lantern was a great black horse, head up and ears pricked forward, but standing as still as a statue. Then Sheridan saw Jim slumped down in the saddle with his eyes closed. He shouted to the other men and they all hurried out of the ranch house.

" Jim's been hurt," Sheridan exclaimed, " but he

found Black Tiger and the horse brought him home."

Quickly the men lifted Jim from the saddle and carried him into the house. Then John said to Buck Davis, " It's going to storm. Take Tiger to the stable. We'll take care of Jim."

Buck led Tiger to the stable and took the saddle from his back. He saw that the horse was breathing easily and had evidently been walking for some time.

When Buck came back, John said, " Is Tiger all right? "

" Yes," said Buck. " He was breathing easy. Looks as if he's been only walking. The storm will strike any minute now. Tiger got Jim here just in time."

Meanwhile, Jim was lying on his bunk, and one of the men got some cold water and bathed his face. At this, Jim opened his eyes and became really conscious for the first time since the accident. But he was still too weak to talk.

All the men were gathered around Jim when the first sharp crack of thunder came. There was another, still nearer, and then one crash followed another. The wind and rain began to beat upon the house. Water streamed in torrents down the window-panes and the storm roared in ever increasing violence.

All the men were thinking the same thing—if Jim had been on an ordinary horse, the animal would have been afraid of the coming storm and would suddenly have started galloping for home. Jim, in his unconscious state, would have been thrown to the ground, and now would be lying out there somewhere on the wild range with this deluge of rain beating down upon him. They knew that, in spite of the coming storm, Tiger had kept himself to a walk, for Jim could not have stayed in the saddle at any faster pace. How far Tiger had walked with Jim unconscious on his back, they had, of course, no way of knowing.

For two hours the storm roared on with unabated fury. At last it began to lessen, and the rain came only now and then in fitful gusts against the windows of the ranch-house. By this time Jim felt able to tell the men what had happened. He described how Tiger had attacked the horse thieves hiding in the underbrush and how he had driven them away. Then he told how Tiger had been frightened when the big wolf leaped out into the trail, but he could not remember anything after that. But the men had already discovered the bad bruise on the side of Jim's head, and from it they could guess very well what had happened.

Jim fell asleep and slept peacefully until morning. Although he was still weak and pale, he got up with the other men and went outside in the bright sunlight. Buck Davis had already opened the stable door and Tiger was out in the yard. When he saw Jim coming, the black horse at once came up to him, making friendly sounds. Jim smiled and rubbed Tiger on the neck.

At this moment Pete, the cook, came out and handed Jim some hard biscuits. " Here, Jim," he said, " you know Tiger likes the hard ones."

While Jim fed Tiger the biscuits, the other men all stood around, patting him, brushing down his sleek black coat with their hands, and telling him what a fine horse he was. Tiger could not understand their words, but he could understand the friendly sound of their voices. Best of all, he knew he was with Jim again and Jim no longer was acting strangely as he had in the night.

When the last biscuit was gone, Jim threw one arm around his horse's neck, and Black Tiger bent his head to rub his soft nose against Jim's shoulder. The big black horse knew that he was back at last with the master he loved.

THE END

1